SANTA'S SEVEN-DAY BABY TUTORIAL

BY
MEG MAXWELL

MILLS BOON

First Published in Great Britain 2017
By Mills & Boon, an imprint of HarperCollins*Publishers*
1 London Bridge Street, London, SE1 9GF

© 2017 Meg Maxwell

ISBN: 978-0-263-92348-3

23-1117

Our policy is to use papers that are natural, renewable and recyclable products and made from wood grown in sustainable forests. The logging and manufacturing processes conform to the legal environmental regulations of the country of origin.

Printed and bound in Spain
by CPI, Barcelona

Meg Maxwell lives on the coast of Maine with her teenage son, their beagle and their black-and-white cat. When she's not writing, Meg is either reading, at the movies or thinking up new story ideas on her favourite little beach (even in winter) just minutes from her house. Interesting fact: Meg Maxwell is a pseudonym for author Melissa Senate, whose women's fiction titles have been published in over twenty-five countries.

Dedicated with appreciation to my readers.
Thank you.

Chapter One

Fbi agent Colt Asher's new mission: infiltrate an Amish village and recoup a stolen black-and-white guinea pig named Sparkles.

What Colt should be doing right now was planning his vacation, some much-needed R & R, maybe on the Gulf of Mexico or a trip to New Orleans for some beignets and good bourbon. Or he could dust off his passport and take off for France. Italy. Germany. Practice his Spanish in Madrid. Instead, late in the afternoon on the day before his two-week vacation would start, his boss, Harlan Holtzman, had called Colt into his office with a special request.

Yesterday, Harlan had taken his eight-year-old niece out to lunch for her birthday in their hometown, Grass Creek, a suburb of Houston, where the FBI office was located. On the way to the pizzeria, the girl had spot-

ted a black-and-white guinea pig in the window of the
pet shop and wistfully said her birthday and Christmas
wish combined was to have that guinea pig for her very
own and she'd name it Sparkles and take good care of
it. Harlan, the old softy, planned to surprise the girl.
So this afternoon he'd gone back to the pet shop and
bought the critter and a bunch of whatever guinea pigs
needed, like a cage and wood shavings and hidey tun-
nels. He then set down Sparkles in his new cage on the
curb near his pickup while he went back in the store to
collect the huge bag of shavings and guinea-pig pellets.
A clerk had then talked his ear off about proper care
of the critter and got him to add a book called *Caring
for Your New Guinea Pig* to the bundle.

"A twenty-four-dollar Christmas present ended up
costing me over one hundred and fifty bucks!" Harlan muttered.

Bigger problem: when Harlan finally came out to the
truck with the shavings and pellets and book, Sparkles
and his cage were gone. A guinea-pig thief in Grass
Creek? Most unusual. The boss asked around, and one
woman reported that she did see an Amish girl with
red pigtails take the cage off the curb and put it in her
buggy sometime before it moved on, but the woman
hadn't realized she was witnessing a theft. According
to her statement: *I mean, the Amish don't steal, right?*

Apparently, they did. Or this one girl did, anyway.

What *wasn't* unusual was seeing Amish folks in
Grass Creek. The Amish community was about ten
minutes away from the large town with its bustling
center, where Amish folks had a very popular indoor
market to sell their baked goods, wares and handcrafted furniture. Though Colt lived fifteen minutes

away in Houston, he'd gone to the Amish market for all the tables in his condo, and last spring, when he wanted to buy two cribs for his then pregnant-with-twins sister, he wouldn't have shopped anywhere else. The craftsmanship was impeccable. Colt also never passed the stall with the Amish-baked lemon scones and sourdough bread without buying enough to stuff his freezer. There were always several Amish buggies around Grass Creek every day. He'd never been to the Amish community itself. But if there was one thing Colt knew from ten years as an FBI agent, it was that anyone, even an Amish girl with red braids and a bonnet, was capable of anything. Colt had arrested men who looked like bad guys in action movies and he'd arrested the most angelic-looking women who you'd never suspect of a thing.

Guard up, always. That was Colt's motto. It had to be.

His guard hadn't been up on his last case. He needed this vacation to clear his head, to forget what had happened. But there was something he'd never forget: that one of those angelic-looking women had managed to con him and betray him and it would never, ever happen again.

"I wouldn't ask you to drive out there, Colt," Harlan said. "But Jones and Cametti just left on the gun-running case, and I've got that damn fund-raiser dinner I can't get out of, and since your vacation technically doesn't start until you leave tonight, I can ask you while you're still here and not feel that guilty."

Colt laughed. "No problem, Harlan. I'll have Sparkles at your house in a couple hours." A drive out to all that farmland and fresh air was probably just what he needed. A perfect start to R & R.

"Appreciate it, Colt. Thank you."

He'd drive to the Amish village, flash his badge around and ask about a red-haired girl who'd been to town today, recover the guinea pig and drop him off at Harlan's, and then he'd pack his bags and throw a dart at the world map hanging in his living room. Where it landed was where he'd go to forget that disaster of a last case...and remember.

As Jordan Lapp's buggy came around the curve in the road, Anna Miller glanced up from the calf she was bottle-feeding in the barn of her farmhouse and sent up a prayer: *Please, please, please do not be here to propose.*

She was twenty-four. And unmarried. Spinster age for an Amish woman. Over the past five years, she'd turned down ten potential suitors and the eight marriage proposals that had come anyway. Some of those proposals were more about her being the right age and not married. Some of the men had truly liked her. One had loved her, and she'd broken his heart, which had broken hers.

Anna had always hoped that the undeniable fact that she was "different" would make her unappealing to the men of her community. It hadn't. She was outspoken. She talked too much about what she read in novels and nonfiction. She didn't understand why cooking and laundry were "women's work." She wore overalls instead of dresses to do her barn chores and paint the handcrafted furniture their community produced. Orphaned when her mother passed away two years ago, she lived alone, unusual for the Amish, but her *onkel* Eli preferred she live in her family home and not with him and her *aenti* Kate because Anna was a "bad influence" on their eight-year-old daughter, Sadie.

Her matchmaking *onkel* had promised a few of her would-be suitors a horse or furniture to sell if they would propose to Anna. The man was a well-meaning busybody, but Anna knew he was operating more out of love for his wife, who worried about Anna incessantly, than out of a need to control his niece. All the proposals had been turned down, infuriating her uncle, irritating her aunt and earning an "unacceptable" respect from her young cousin, Sadie.

"Cousin Anna is her own woman," Sadie had said with pride in her voice over lunch one afternoon, her new favorite novel, *Anne of Green Gables*, on the table beside her sandwich.

Sadie's mother had raised an eyebrow but had said nothing, which was telling. Anna *was* her own woman. Consequence: Anna was also alone. Sadie's mother would allow her young daughter to see for herself how Anna's choices affected her. Anna admired that about her aunt, even if Kate was making a point. Of course, Sadie was being raised Amish and attended church and followed the *Ordnung*, the rules of behavior. But Sadie read widely, just as Anna always had. Her cousin's heart—and head—would guide her, just as Anna's had.

Jordan emerged from the buggy. Uh-oh: he was in his church clothes, a black jacket and pants, a black straw hat. He stopped in front of her, patted the calf, and smiled nervously. "Anna, here's the thing. The past couple of months, I've sent my brother and a cousin to ask you if you'd date me. You told them no. So I'm going against tradition here to cut to the chase. Will you marry me?" He pulled a miniature wooden clock from his jacket pocket. He likely made the clock himself, for this very purpose. The Amish did not propose with diamond rings.

Her heart plummeted. She liked Jordan. He was kind and had beautiful blue eyes. She hated to hurt his feelings or his pride or even deny him whatever it was her *onkel* may have promised him. "Jordan, you're a very *gut* man, but I'm sorry that I must turn down your kind proposal. I'm not looking to marry."

Jordan frowned. "What else is there? Are you just going to nurse the sick calves and paint furniture until you're old? Who will love you? Care for you? You'll have no children."

She did want children. She also wanted a husband. She just wasn't so sure she could commit to an Amish man, which meant committing to being Amish, to living here for the rest of her life. There was a big world out there. Or even just the town of Grass Creek—a world of difference from their Amish village.

"I don't have all the answers," she said. "I'm sorry, Jordan. Were I looking to marry, you would make a wonderful husband."

He sighed. "Well, if you change your mind by day's end, let me know. Otherwise I'll date Abigail. She speaks her mind as you do. I like that."

She smiled. Good for him. "I won't change my mind. Go date Abigail." Her friend from childhood had a crush on Jordan and would be very happy to date him with the unspoken intention of marriage. That was how it worked in the Amish community. You liked who you liked and if you started dating it was because you planned to become engaged.

"You won't tell her I proposed to you?" he asked.

"Of course not."

He nodded, put the clock back in his pocket, and left.

Anna watched his buggy round the bend and heard a twig snap on the other side of the barn. Someone had been eavesdropping.

"Anna Miller, your mother would not approve."

Drat. Her *aenti* was here. And apparently had heard the entire exchange.

The calf's bottle empty, Anna stood up just as Kate Miller rounded the barn with a basket in her hand. Her dear *aenti* often brought Anna lunch when she made the afternoon meal for her family.

"Chicken soup, sourdough bread and strawberry preserves," Kate said, handing over the basket. She frowned at the sight of Anna in her denim overalls and baseball cap, paint stain on one thigh. Kate wore the traditional calf-length modest dress and a black bonnet, which symbolized that she was married. Single women in their village wore white bonnets. Anna's baseball cap was blue.

"Thank you, *Aenti*," Anna said, the aroma of the soup and fresh-baked bread making her stomach growl.

"Is Sadie here?" Kate asked. "She ran off after we returned from Grass Creek but I didn't see her as I walked over."

Anna glanced out the barn doors for a sight of her young cousin. "I haven't seen her, either. Shall I send her home if I do?"

Her *aenti* nodded. "I have some sewing chores for her."

It was no wonder her cousin had run off for a little freedom while she could get it. Anna's aunt believed that idle hands made for a wayward mind, so she tried to keep the eight-year-old occupied with chores so that young Sadie wouldn't be able to spend too much time with her cousin Anna.

"Anna, I try to understand you," Kate said. "But it's been two years since your *mamm* passed. You won't date anyone. You turn down good marriage proposals that come anyway. You are meant to be a wife and mother, Anna—if you are Amish."

If. If. If. Anna had not yet been baptized in the faith.

"I don't want to make you feel bad, Anna. But you're setting a terrible example for the *kinder*. There are only eleven families in our village and lots of *kinder*. Including your very impressionable cousin. Sadie said just this morning that she wants to be just like cousin Anna when she grows up. Imagine if your *onkel* had heard that!"

Sadie would likely not be allowed to go to Anna's house anymore at all.

Her *aenti* lifted her chin. "I think you should leave, Anna."

Anna gasped. "What?"

"Take your long-put-off *rumspringa*," Kate said. "You didn't have the chance when it was customary. Discover once and for all if you want to be Amish or not." With that, her aunt turned and headed back up the road to her home, a quarter mile away.

Her *rumspringa*. All during her childhood, Anna had watched the boys and girls of her village reach fourteen, fifteen or sixteen and have their *rumspringa*, the time when Amish teenagers could experience life

as an "Englisher" with no consequences for their behavior and choices, to a degree, of course, and then
commit—or not—to their Amish faith. It was then that
they would be baptized into the faith, committing to the
Amish lifestyle and *Ordnung.* As a girl, Anna had lived
for that time to come, anticipating, waiting, dreaming. Whenever she'd gotten a chance to go into Grass
Creek, she'd watch the Englishers—so named for the
language they spoke, as opposed to the Pennsylvania Dutch of the Amish—studying how they dressed,
the shoes they wore, the jewelry, all forbidden to the
Amish, that decorated their necks and wrists and ears.
Earlier this afternoon, when Anna had gone to Grass
Creek with her family to deliver new furniture to their
market stall, a woman approached wearing bright red
lipstick and long dangling silver earrings, and Anna
had been mesmerized by the glamour—the very opposite of plain, as Amish were supposed to be.

She'd rarely been in cars, except for taxis and ambu-
lances. She'd never listened to music through the ear-
phones she saw so many people wearing, never held a
cell phone or looked up anything on the internet. She'd
never seen *Gilmore Girls* or *Casablanca* or *The Simp-
sons,* shows and movies she only knew about through
magazines she'd flipped through in town and books,
which were her lifeline, along with people watching
and listening. There was a great big world out there.
And during her *rumspringa* she'd get to experience
it all.

But then her dear *daed* had been killed in a freak
farm accident when Anna was fifteen, so she'd put
off her *rumspringa.* She was an only child, rare in the
Amish world, but her parents hadn't been blessed with

other children. Two years later, just as Anna was ready to take off her head covering and use, for the first time, the internet via the Grass Creek library's community computers, her beloved *mamm* got sick. Cancer. Anna had cared for her frail mother for five years before she passed. Anna was so grief-stricken, so lost without her *mamm*, that she'd retreated into herself, taking care of the sickly calves, painting the furniture the men of the community had built. And turned down guy after guy, proposal after proposal. Now she was twenty-four and still here. One foot out. One foot in. And not moving. But always wondering. Dreaming.

"My own *rumspringa* was a disappointment," her mother had once told her. "There is almost too much choice, too much technology, too *much* out there. Here it is quiet and peaceful and you use only what you truly need. It's a good way to experience the meaning of life, Anna."

Anna's heart squeezed with the thought of her mother, but just then she saw a pair of red pigtails fly past the barn. Spending time with her whirlwind of a cousin always lifted Anna's mood. The girl was probably hiding from her *mamm* for a bit.

Anna was about to enter the barn to find Sadie when a black SUV came down the road, a man behind the wheel. Anna's house was the first one from the main road, so perhaps he wanted to inquire about furniture or horse training or just gawk at the "plain people." The man parked the car and got out and looked around, his gaze landing on hers.

She sucked in a breath. He was tall, over six feet, with a broad chest and narrow hips. He wore a long-sleeved button-down shirt and charcoal pants, and was clean-shaven, with a bit of five-o'clock shadow. His thick dark hair was swept back like the movie stars whose photos she saw on posters at the theater in Grass Creek. And his eyes were green. He was the most handsome man she'd ever seen. And she'd seen her share of Englishers in town.

He was carrying something in his right hand. She peered more closely to see what it was. A wallet? No—it was a badge.

She froze. Police? What would an officer of the law want with their community?

Chapter Two

As the man approached, Anna could more clearly see the badge. FBI. She felt him assessing her from head to toe, taking in the overalls, the baseball cap.

"Hi there," he said, holding up the badge. "My name is Colt Asher. I'm an agent with the FBI's Houston office. A woman reported seeing an Amish girl with red pigtails take a guinea pig in a cage off the curb in front of Grass Creek Pets about two hours ago. I need to have that guinea pig back."

Anna tilted her head. "I thought government agents handled kidnappings and drugs and organized crime."

"And stolen guinea pigs when the victim is my boss," he said with a smile. "It's his niece's birthday *and* Christmas present."

Oh, boy. "Did you say the perpetrator had red pigtails?" she asked, hoping she'd misheard but knowing full well she had not. There was only one girl in the village with red hair. Her eight-year-old cousin.

He took a small leather notebook from his pocket and flipped through it. "Red braided pigtails."

Oh, Sadie. Her cousin knew stealing was wrong. The Ten Commandments were printed on a huge plaque in the kitchen of the girl's house. Lately, Sadie had been full of questions about the English and how they lived. Earlier this afternoon, when they'd been at the market, Anna had watched her cousin studying a girl who was looking at a doll cradle that Anna herself had painted a pretty yellow with tiny white stars. Anna could see the wistfulness in Sadie's eyes as she'd taken in the girl's red light-up sneakers with bright orange laces. Orange was frowned upon in their community. Too flashy. Forget about the light-up part. But would Sadie take a guinea pig to have something from the English world? Maybe.

Anna glanced around. No one in the vicinity. No buggies heading into town or coming back. It was possible no one had seen the car drive in. That was good. Otherwise, there would be questions. Sadie and her family could get in terrible trouble with the bishop if Sadie had indeed taken something that did not belong to her.

The handsome FBI agent was watching her. She could almost feel him taking her stats, measuring her composure. Suspects had to crack under that pressure.

"Follow me, please," she said and led the way into the barn, which was bigger than the house. Three calves, on the mend and ready to be returned to their owners, were chewing at hay, and glanced at her as she entered with the agent. She set her basket lunch on a table near the door.

The barn was silent. But she had a feeling her cousin was here.

"Sadie?" she called. "Are you here?"

"*Ja*, I am here," a small voice answered as the girl stepped from behind a pen at the back of the barn. But Sadie didn't come forward and stood very straight.

"Sadie, this is Colt Asher. He's an FBI agent and—"

Sadie burst into tears. "I'm sorry! I didn't mean to take the furry little thing. Well, I did, because I did take him, but I didn't mean to. He was all alone in the cage on the sidewalk. I thought someone abandoned him. I watched him for ten minutes and he kept twitching his nose at me as though he was trying to say 'Take me home, Sadie.' So I picked up his cage and put it into the buggy when no one was looking and brought him here."

"Here?" Anna repeated, moving closer, aware that the agent was staying back. "As in our village or here as in my barn?"

Sadie bit her lip, then moved to the right and pushed aside a hay bale. A small metal cage with a black-and-white guinea pig was on the floor. The rodent, nibbling a lettuce leaf, looked at them and twitched his nose.

Sadie looked down at her feet. "I'm sorry. I really am."

"Sadie," Anna said, "even if you thought he was abandoned on the sidewalk, you should have asked permission to take him—from the pet-shop owners, from your parents."

Sadie hung her head. "I know, cousin. I'm sorry. I'll

wait with the FBI agent so you can get my *mamm* and *daed* and tell them what I did."

Anna kneeled down in front of her niece and took her hands. "Sadie Miller, I will do no such thing. But I want you to promise that you will never, ever take something that does not belong to you. I am trusting you. And holding you to your word."

Sadie looked up at Anna and then threw her arms around her. "I promise, cousin. I promise with all my heart." She turned to Colt Asher. "Will you take me to jail now?"

Colt approached Sadie and also kneeled down in front of her. "Nope."

Sadie tilted her head. "What is *nope*?"

"It's a nice English way of saying no," Anna explained.

"Oh," Sadie said. "Nope," she repeated, trying out the word. "Nope. Nope, I won't ever take anything that doesn't belong to me."

The agent smiled. "You promised and that's good enough for me. But I do have to bring Sparkles back to his rightful owner. He's a little girl's Christmas present."

"Sparkles?" Sadie wiped her tears away and smiled. "That's a good name."

"So is Sadie," he said, standing up. He turned to Anna. "And your name is Cousin?"

Anna smiled. "No. It's Anna. Anna Miller. The word for *cousin* is a bit difficult to pronounce in Pennsylvania Dutch, so Sadie has always called me cousin. Our community is English-speaking, but we always use certain Pennsylvania-Dutch words. The language evolved from German settlers to colonial Pennsylvania, and Amish communities across the country use it. For Mother and Father—*Mamm* and *Daed*—for example. *Gut* for good. *Ja* for yes." Why was she rambling? Because the man was so close and so good-looking and green-eyed that her stomach was fluttering. When was the last time a man's presence had made her feel anything? Maybe never.

Sadie handed over Sparkles's cage to the agent. "He sure is cute."

"Ja," Colt said, and both Sadie and Anna burst into grins. "He is. Looks like you took care of him."

"I'm really sorry," Sadie said again, then threw her arms around Anna for a few seconds and fled.

The agent watched her run off, then turned back to Anna. "Sometimes, all's well that ends well."

Anna smiled. "Shakespeare. I recently read that play."

The sunlight streaming in the open doors of the barn lit the agent's lush dark hair and his forearms, which were strong and muscular. She could stare at him all day. There was a slight cleft in his chin. "So you're Sadie's cousin but you're not Amish?" he asked.

"I am Amish."

He looked confused, and she realized she was in her barn clothes instead of the usual long dress and head covering. "These are my *daed's* old overalls. I wear them when I'm caring for the calves or painting furniture that our community makes to sell at market in Grass Creek."

"Ah, now I understand. My line of work doesn't bring me into contact with the Amish so I don't know all that much about your culture. I suppose I'm just used to seeing Amish women in long dresses and bonnets."

For a moment, they stared at each other. Anna couldn't take her eyes off the man, and granted, she had earned the unfortunate nickname of Fanciful Anna, but he seemed unable to look away from her, as well. While wearing coveralls and a baseball cap and smelling like the barn? She almost laughed. Fanciful Anna, indeed.

"Agent Asher, I'm sorry that your time was taken up by this. And I appreciate your kindness to my cousin. I think she was overcome with desire to have something from the English world. Not that I'm excusing her behavior. But I do try to understand Sadie so that I can better guide her."

"Colt," he said. "Well, the moment I return Sparkles, I'm on vacation, so no worries about my time."

"Vacation," she repeated, hearing the wistfulness in her own voice. "Are you going somewhere special?"

"I haven't decided. I have two weeks off, so the first ten days or so I plan to spend somewhere amazing, like Rome or Machu Picchu or a Hawaiian island."

She sighed. "I would love to eat pasta in Rome." She imagined herself tossing coins in the Trevi Fountain. Seeing the Colosseum with her own eyes.

He smiled. "Vacation coming up?"

She shook her head. "The Amish don't vacation. It's not our way to spend money on such things. Sunday is our day of rest and that's plenty." She turned to the acres of farmland, which always made her feel connected to the world. Usually. "I've never been beyond Grass Creek...well, except for the hospital in Houston. I've read about all the places you've mentioned, though. Must be hard to come back home from such special destinations."

"Well, wherever I go, I am actually looking forward to returning to Texas since I'll be spending a few days visiting with my twin brother and his family. I was adopted as a baby and just discovered he existed a few months ago. I'm still grappling with it a bit, to be honest."

Anna gasped. "I have a cousin I didn't know existed until a few months ago. She was shunned before I was born and she fled the community. She was only seventeen."

"Shunned?" Colt said. "What did she do?"

Anna shrugged. "No one will talk about it. But it's not hard to break the rules of our community. It makes me very sad to think about, though. I wonder if she misses us. She must."

"I'm sure she does," he said. "I met my twin brother, just briefly, for the first time back in May. Turns out he didn't know about my existence until recently, either. I've thought about him so much these past few months. I can't imagine your cousin doesn't miss all of you like crazy. And she never even got to meet you."

Lately, Anna often thought about her cousin Mara. Her aunt and uncle never talked about their niece, but Anna had found some of her things while helping to clear out Kate and Eli's attic, and her *aenti* had finally told Anna about Mara.

"Is your twin brother your only sibling?" she asked to change the subject. She didn't want to talk about herself. She would much prefer to learn more about Colt Asher.

"I have a sister. She was also adopted by my parents. She's married with twin boys herself. They're seven months old now. Very cute." He gestured at her painting area in the back corner of the barn. "I see you're painting a cradle. I bought my sister cribs from the Amish market in Grass Creek."

She smiled. "I might have done the finishing. I love working on baby furniture. I have a special weakness for infants. The past couple of months I've been helping to care for the Sanderson triplets. Their parents have three young ones and now three babies."

"Must be a noisy house. It's quiet here," he said, glancing around. From his expression, she could see that he appreciated the quiet and the land. The Amish community stretched for miles in this rural area, and Anna could barely see the roof of her *aenti* and *onkel's* house in the near distance. Sometimes she loved the solitude, when it was just her and her thoughts and her books. But other times, she yearned for conversations like this one, where she'd hear things she'd only read about.

"*Ja.* I live alone. My parents are gone. It's just me now. Do you live in Grass Creek?" She wanted to know everything about him. A glance at his left hand told her he wasn't married. She wondered if he had a girlfriend. Or a fiancée. Sex before marriage was forbidden in her community, but it wasn't in his world. Her thoughts traveled in a direction that made her toes tingle and her cheeks flame. His hard chest, flat stomach and muscles were obvious through the shirt he wore.

"Next door, in Houston," he said, reminding her that she'd asked a question and shouldn't be ogling the man. "In a skyscraper condo on the thirty-second floor."

She sighed again, this time inwardly. He lived in the sky and chased bad guys for a living. He was unlike anyone she knew. Anyone she'd ever know…here. But he was like her, too. He had close family he didn't know—his twin brother. Just like she had close family she didn't know, her cousin Mara. She wished she could talk to him more about that, over coffee. But she couldn't exactly invite the man inside her home. His car had been parked by her barn long enough that someone must have spotted it. She had no doubt they were being watched by the curious and the worried.

Ignore them, she told herself. *This gorgeous specimen of a man is here, right now, so talk to him while you can.*

"The thirty-second floor," she said, imagining being in a building that high up, looking out on the lights of a city like Houston. "That sounds wonderful. I've always dreamed of seeing the world outside this village, outside of Grass Creek. My aunt, Sadie's mother, thinks I should take my long-put-off *rumspringa*—experience life as an Englisher—so I can commit or not to the faith."

"Why don't you?" he asked.

Before she could respond, one of the calves mooed and she realized she still had one more calf to feed. She could stand here and talk to the agent all day. Stare at the agent all day. But why prolong this? He would leave any minute now and she would never see him again unless she happened to cross his path at the Amish market. Fanciful Anna needed to be realistic, as her *aenti* and *onkel* always said. "I'd better feed the little guy or he'll come charging. Which is good—he's in perfect health now and ready to go home."

The agent nodded—and held her gaze a beat longer than the usual. She wasn't imagining his attraction to her, coveralls and paint stains and calf poop and all. This interaction with the agent would sustain her a good long time. No matter how unsettled she might be feeling about her life and what she wanted, her thoughts were her own and now they'd be filled with this man.

"And I'd better get Sparkles back," he said. "Thank you again for your help. You handled the situation very kindly."

Neither of them moved.

She glanced at Sparkles in his cage. Brought together by a black-and-white guinea pig, she thought with a smile. "If you don't mind, I'd like to cover the cage from prying eyes."

He nodded and she found a large cloth. "Merry Christmas, sweet Sparkles," she said to the critter, then covered the cage. He took it in his right hand, gave her something of a smile and then held the cage in front of him as he walked to his car. She stood in the doorway of the barn, watching him go. Wishing he could stay. He quickly put the cage in the back, then glanced toward her and held up a hand.

She held up hers. Then he got inside and drove back up the dirt road, leaving her strangely bereft.

Any moment now, her entire village would descend on her, curious about what the Englisher wanted with them. She would say it had to do with a missing pet and she'd explain that none of the villagers was missing a pet. Not the truth, exactly, but not a lie.

She watched the agent's car disappear up the long drive, then she closed her eyes to commit everything about him to memory.

After dropping off Sparkles with the boss's relieved wife, Colt was officially on vacation. The muscles in his shoulders relaxed just a bit. He stood in front of the world map in his living room and tried to settle on a destination. Europe? Asia? Stick closer to home? Someplace warm like the Florida Keys, maybe.

He couldn't decide because he was distracted. And not by the last case or the deceitful woman who'd managed to con him.

But by Anna Miller. The Amish woman. Her inquisitive pale brown eyes and pink-red lips, which were unadorned. The long blond braid that fell down past her shoulders almost to her waist. Her curiosity. The way she'd listened so intently.

His intercom system buzzed, jarring him out of his thoughts. His doorman informed him his sister and her husband were on their way up. That was weird. Cathy and Chris lived just a few miles away and weren't the "stop by" kind of people. The parents of seven-month-old twins, they were regimented to a fault—they planned, made lists and scheduled their lives around sleep times.

The doorbell rang and he opened the door; his sister wheeled in the twins in their double stroller, while her husband carried a small suitcase and a huge tote bag. The two of them looked harried. Thirty-year-old Cathy seemed on the verge of tears, and Chris looked exhausted, like he'd been up all night with babies. Probably had been.

"Remember when we spoke this morning, you mentioned you hadn't picked a vacation destination yet and had no tickets booked anywhere?" Cathy asked, a small glob of what looked and smelled like peach puree on her shoulder.

He narrowed his eyes at her. "I remember."

"Our nanny just canceled on us!" Cathy said, tears

glistening in her eyes. "She had the dates of our cruise wrong and now she can't watch the twins for the week. She's wonderful—not just a neighbor we've known for years, but a loving, fun grandmother with so much experience."

Oh, God. He was beginning to see where this was going.

"We haven't been away from the boys in seven months," Cathy said. "The cruise is our Christmas present to each other and we board in three hours. We'll have to cancel unless…"

He stared at Cathy. He stared at Chris.

No. No, no. This couldn't be happening. He loved his nephews, but his experience at babysitting had been limited to an hour here and there while visiting so his sister could get some treadmill time or watch a TV show and his brother-in-law could tinker with his car. Watching the twins in their family room, all baby-proofed and set up with foam pads and crawling areas and toys, when their parents were screaming distance away, was a piece of cake.

But Cathy was asking him to babysit two seven-month-olds for an entire week.

It was almost funny.

"Pleeeease," Cathy begged.

"Please. God, please," his brother-in-law added.

Colt's stomach twisted. He glanced at Noah on the left side of the stroller. The very cute tyke was chewing some kind of cloth-like book with pictures of monkeys. Nathaniel, equally adorable on the right, was picking up what looked like Cheerios from the tray table and examining them. He flung one and giggled.

Cathy stepped in front of the stroller, blocking them

and their criminal ways. "It's just seven days, Colt. You'll still have a solid week left of your vacation to recuperate."

Just seven days. *Just* seven days?

"Merry Christmas?" his sister said, pleading with her eyes. He had a mental montage of all the times his sister had been there for him from the time they were little. She and her husband needed a break, he had the time and so that was that.

"Merry Christmas," Colt said on a sigh.

The relief on his brother-in-law's face almost made Colt smile. Chris dropped the suitcase and tote on the floor near the stroller and gave his shoulder a good rotation.

"We left the car seats in the lobby with the doorman," Cathy said. "And everything else you need is in there," she added, pointing to the bags. "Plus their schedule and all the pertinent information. They're fed, changed and ready for a nap, so at least your vacation will start sort of restfully." She spent a good five minutes going over what to do in an emergency, which was also detailed in a list in the tote bag. Finally, she threw her arms around him. "I owe you," she added, then she and Chris booked out before Colt could even say "bon voyage."

"Well, guys," Colt said to the twins, one still chewing his book, one now alternating between eating his Cheerios and throwing them. "It's just the three of us. For a week."

He could handle this. He was thirty-two years old. He was an FBI agent with ten years' experience under his belt. He'd taken down ruthless criminals. He'd found a missing guinea pig in record time. He could take care of two cute babies, his own nephews, for a week.

Noah, older by one and a half minutes, started fussing, his face crumbling into a combination of discomfort and rage. Uh-oh. He flung his little book and started wiggling his arms. Colt unbuckled his harness and took him out of the stroller, praying the tyke would smell like his usual baby shampoo and baby lotion, and not like a baby who needed to be changed.

He hoisted Noah in his arms and the baby squeezed his chin. "Good grip, kid," he said, trying to sound soothing, the way his brother-in-law always did. He bounced Noah a bit and the baby seemed to like that. He visited his nephews once a month or so, dropping by with little gifts, but never stayed very long. He really had no idea how to take care of a baby, let alone two, but he could follow directions.

He carefully kneeled down with Noah in one arm to open the tote bag. He saw bottles and formula and diapers and ointment and pacifiers and teething toys and little stuffed animals. In the suitcase was clothing and blankets. He found the schedule, which was a mile long. Lots of baby lingo. This wasn't going to be easy.

He pulled out his phone and called his sister. "Cathy, I've got the schedule in my hand. Are you sure I can do this?"

"Absolutely," his sister said with conviction. "Don't worry, Colt. If you're confused, just remember that they'll tell you what they need."

"Um, Cathy? They don't talk."

"Yes, but they cry. And if they cry, they're either hungry, need changing, are tired, want their lovies, want their pacifiers or want to be picked up. Or they want to crawl."

"And how do I know what cry means what?" Colt asked, eyeing the baby in his arms. Noah was now examining Colt's ear, giving the lobe little tugs.

"Trial and error. In a few hours, you'll just know. Oooh, Colt, we're at the ship! 'Bye now!"

Noah's fascination with his uncle's ear stopped suddenly. He began fussing and wiggling. His face crumpled. Then the wailing started. Man, that was a loud sound from such a tiny child. A sniff in the direction of the baby's padded bottom told Colt he didn't need changing. His sister had said they were fed right before they'd left home. He tried bouncing him a little, but that made the little guy fuss harder. He was stretching out his little arms. Should he set him down to crawl? On the hardwood floor?

Suddenly, an earsplitting shriek came from the stroller. Nathaniel was holding up his arms, his little face angry.

Well, he couldn't pick up Nathaniel with Noah in his arms. He put Noah back in the stroller and reclined the seat, then handed Noah a pacifier. The baby immediately settled down, his big blue eyes getting droopy. Success! Except that his brother's cries were going to keep him from his nap. Colt quickly took Nathaniel out of the stroller, bounced him against his chest for a few minutes until the baby quieted, then settled him back in the stroller, reclined the seat, popped a pacifier in his mouth and his eyes began drifting shut, too. He remembered from a visit to his sister's house that the boys liked falling asleep to their lullaby player, so he poked around the tote until he found it and hung it on the stroller, Brahms's Lullaby playing softy.

The knots were back in Colt's shoulders. He'd handled this okay, but what about when they woke up and *both* needed changing. Feeding. Burping. And all that other baby stuff. How would he know what to do and when? He could hire a nanny, a baby nurse, to help out for the week. He sat down at his desk in front of his laptop and typed "nanny services" into the search engine and a bunch popped up. After calling several he learned that no one had anyone available on such short notice and especially so close to Christmas. One service had a trainee available with no experience, but that was Colt himself, so little good that would do.

He was going to need help. Suddenly, the Amish woman's pretty face popped into his mind again. Hadn't she said she loved babies? Hadn't she been helping to take care of infant triplets for the past two months? Add to that the way she'd been so kind to her little cousin when that could have turned out very differently for the girl. And the way Anna had listened to him talk about his life, as though it was the most exciting thing she'd ever heard, though it probably was.

The way she dreamed of experiencing life outside her village. Perhaps being his nanny could be her... what had she called it? *Rumspringa*. She'd get to live as an "Englisher." He'd get a homespun nanny.

He grabbed his phone and then realized he didn't have a telephone number for her, and he was pretty sure the Amish didn't have telephones in their homes. Which meant a drive back to the Amish village.

Now he just had to manage to get Noah and Nathaniel in their car seats without waking them up. The odds were not in his favor.

Chapter Three

Just over two hours after her conversation with Colt Asher, Anna still could not stop thinking about him—his handsome face, the thick, silky dark hair, his green eyes, the slight cleft in his chin and how tall and fit he was. She and her *aenti*, *onkel* and young cousin were in the barn, Kate and Sadie wrapping the painted furniture that Anna and Eli were loading into the pony wagon parked outside. Thinking of the FBI agent in his condo in the sky made the chore of lugging furniture much more enjoyable.

As Anna and her *onkel* carried the bureau, a black SUV came down the long dirt drive into their village.

Colt was back. Goose bumps rose on every bit of her body at the idea of seeing him again.

But why was he here? Was there a problem with the

guinea pig? Had he changed his mind about Sadie's lack of punishment? A flash of fear crawled inside her.

"Is he the same Englisher who was here earlier?" her *onkel* asked as they finished loading the bureau into the wagon.

"Ja," she said, spotting his unforgettable face through the windshield. "I wonder what he wants."

As the FBI agent parked, her *aenti* and cousin emerged from the barn, Sadie wide-eyed.

Colt got out of his car, the engine still running, the windows lowered halfway. "Anna, I was hoping to speak to you."

"About?" her *onkel* asked, stepping forward. "I'm Eli Miller, Anna's uncle."

To the Amish, men were heads of the household, but this was Anna's house and she ran her own life. Something her *onkel* didn't forget but ignored. Still, she wouldn't show disrespect to Eli in front of a stranger. But later, she would let him know she would speak for and answer for herself.

"A job offer," Colt said, his gaze on Anna.

While Anna stared at him, she could see out of the corner of her eye that her cousin and *aenti* were looking at each other with wide eyes.

"A job offer? What do you mean?" Anna asked, stepping forward next to her *onkel*.

"If you come over to my car, you'll see," Colt said, gesturing all of them over to the black SUV.

They all looked at one another, then followed him to the car.

Anna peered in. The front seats were empty. In the back were two car seats, rear-facing. She moved to the back of the car so she could look at the babies. They were about six months old, she'd say, and not identical but did look a lot alike. Both had wispy dark hair and big cheeks. Both were also fast asleep, with little stuffed animals on their laps. One baby had his toy clutched in his tiny fist.

Colt was married? A father? Had she been fantasizing about a married man? He didn't wear a wedding ring, but that didn't mean he wasn't married. Disappointment and shame hit her hard in the stomach.

"Your children are beautiful," Anna said, forcing herself not to sound disappointed.

He smiled and shook his head. "They're not mine. Noah and Nathaniel are my nephews. My sister and her husband were scheduled to leave for a cruise today but their nanny had the dates wrong and couldn't watch the twins. That leaves me as the babysitter."

All four Millers gawked at him. "*You're* the babysitter?" Sadie said with a grin.

"I am. But I could use some help. I would like to hire you, Anna, to be the twins' nanny for the seven days."

Anna was so gobsmacked she could hardly think, let alone speak.

"Not in your home," *Onkel* Eli said to Colt, lifting his chin.

Her *aenti* nodded. "That would not be proper."

"Not in my home," Colt said. "Now that I'm on baby duty, my plan is to visit my twin brother and his wife, who have a newborn. They live in Blue Gulch, a few hours' drive from here. I would book two rooms at an inn downtown, one for me and one for Anna. I will pay her well for her time and expertise."

Onkel Eli was frowning. *Aenti* Kate was thinking— Anna could tell. Sadie's eyes were as big as saucers.

"I accept your offer," Anna said. She wouldn't think about it. She wouldn't ask her *aenti* and *onkel* for their opinions. She was being offered a very good way to have her *rumspringa*, years late, and she would take it.

"Anna, I don't know," *Onkel* Eli said, rubbing his beard. "We don't know this Englisher."

She was taking this job whether overprotective Eli liked it or not. But she could see genuine concern in the man's eyes. "*Onkel*, Colt Asher is an FBI agent in Houston. I will be safe with him."

Colt took his badge from his pocket and showed the Millers, then put it away.

"I think Anna should take the job," her *aenti* said. "This is her opportunity to have her *rumspringa*. To experience life in the English world. Either she will return to us and commit to the *Ordnung* and be baptized in the faith. Or she will not."

Her *onkel* frowned again, but nodded. He extended a hand toward Colt, and Colt shook it.

"The job starts immediately," Colt said. "Or at least I hope it can. I barely survived fifteen minutes on my own. I think I could handle one baby okay. But two? Nope."

"Nope," Sadie repeated with a grin.

One quickly raised eyebrow from her mother let Sadie know that *nope* was not to be added to her vocabulary.

"It's very nice of you to take on the *bopplis* for your sister," Kate said.

Colt tilted his head, and Sadie said, "*Boppli* is Amish for baby."

"*Boppli*," Colt repeated, smiling at Sadie. He looked

at Eli and Kate. "Well, I may not be much of a *boppli*-sitter, but I'd do anything for my sister."

Anna glanced at her *aenti* and could tell the woman liked that response. Both Millers seemed more comfortable by the second with the idea of Anna riding off in a car with a stranger to take a weeklong job.

Except the strain on her aunt's face told Anna that Kate knew her niece might not return. That was the very purpose of this *rumspringa*. To finally know where she belonged. Here? Where she'd been born and raised and lived and worked? Or in the English world, a place and culture she'd only truly experienced in books and magazines?

"Let's help Anna pack quickly," Kate said to Sadie. "We should get her ready to go before the little ones awaken."

Sadie put her hand in Anna's, and the three headed into the house.

What Colt Asher and her *onkel* were talking about outside, Anna could only guess. Furniture. The village. Anna's farm. She would have to make arrangements for the three calves to be moved to their owners; they were ready to be returned anyway.

Anna led the way upstairs to her bedroom. She pulled her suitcase from the closet and set it on her bed, flipping open the top. For a moment Anna just stared at it, the empty suitcase lying open, her entire life about to change.

"Are you sure, Anna?" Kate asked.

Anna nodded. "I'm sure." She looked in her closet. She had many dresses, several inherited from her *mamm*. Her father's two overalls. She had no idea what to pack. Three dresses would do for the week. She moved to her bureau for her undergarments and head coverings and pajama gowns. Would she wear these things while in the English world, though? She had no other clothes.

The suitcase packed in less than a minute, Anna turned to Kate. "Thank for always supporting me, Kate." She hugged her. "You've been wonderful to me."

Kate hugged her back tightly. "I want you to be happy." Then she whispered, "I want you to know where you belong."

Me, too, Anna thought.

"I'll send you postcards, Sadie," Anna told her cousin, kneeling down in front of her.

"Oh *gut*! *Danki*," Sadie said. "I'll miss you so much, Cousin Anna." The little girl wrapped her arms around her. "You're so brave."

For a brave woman, she sure was shaking inside. But she'd never been so excited in her life.

Anna barely knew Colt Asher, but she was pretty sure she detected relief on his handsome face as she got inside his car. He closed the passenger door, then rounded the vehicle. In the rearview mirror, she saw three sets of worried eyes looking at the car. She'd said her goodbyes and it wasn't like the Amish to stand around.

Were the Millers nervous that Anna was leaving? Or that she might not return? Both, most likely. And concerned for little Sadie, who adored her "different" cousin. No matter what happened at the end of the *rum-springa*, Anna would need to take care with the girl.

Colt opened his door and got inside, and once again she could feel him taking her in the way law enforcement officers did. The pale shapeless blue dress with long sleeves and a hem to almost her ankles, the white bonnet, her flat brown boots with laces. She could almost see the notes in his head. *No jewelry. No makeup. Looking straight ahead, ready to go.* And she was ready.

"Not your first time in a car," he remarked, noting that she'd buckled her seat belt. "I hope that's not a ridiculous comment. I have to admit I don't know all that much about the Amish and your practices."

"I've been in a car before. Only a few times. When my *daed* had his accident, my *mamm* used the community telephone to call 911 for an ambulance. We rode with him to the hospital in Houston. I did the same when *Mamm* fell ill. I took taxis back and forth to visit. At first she fought the cancer with chemotherapy, but after a while, there was no hope and she came home." All of it seemed so long ago now.

He started up the long dirt drive to the service road. "I'm sorry. I lost my parents when I was twenty-two. My sister was twenty and in college. For a while it was just the two of us, but then she married and had the little scamps asleep in the back seat. So our family has grown again."

She smiled. "And it's grown even more since you discovered you have a twin brother you never knew existed until just a few months ago. Looks like I'll be getting to know him, too."

"Jake Morrow. He's a rancher in Blue Gulch. He married a woman—the cook at the Full Circle—who recently had a baby, so he's become a father."

"All the *boppli* give the two of you a nice common

ground," Anna said. "Even if you're as different as night and day, you're both giving *kinder* bottles."

He nodded. "That's true. I hadn't even thought of that. We'll be on the same wavelength right now, for sure."

Would *she* be on their wavelength?—that was the question. She hoped so. So far, she and the Englisher talked very easily. "Was your boss relieved to have Sparkles back?"

He laughed. "He was so grateful he added another week to my vacation." But Colt wasn't sure he wanted to be away from the field for too long. Work was his life.

"What my aunt said was true—it's very *gut* of you to spend your vacation caring for your nephews."

"Well, to be honest I was steamrollered into it. But I really would do anything for my sister. And I don't think I could last more than a few days on a beach, diving into waves or sightseeing around a city. The twins will keep me occupied. I need to work and be busy."

"Very Amish," she said with a smile.

He turned to grin at her, and his smile lit up his entire face. "We should get along fine, then."

He was so good-looking, so close, so…*hot*, as the magazines put it, that she had to turn away to collect herself. As they passed through Grass Creek, Anna glanced out the window, noting how the women were dressed. All differently, but in modern clothes. English clothes. Jeans. Skirts. Pants. Brightly colored sweaters. She glanced down at her shapeless blue dress. "I guess when we arrive, everyone will immediately know I'm Amish."

He glanced at her. "You *are* Amish."

"Yes, but I just realized I'd like to start off this *rum-springa* as the person I feel like inside. And this dress and these boots and the head covering…they're all familiar and comforting in a way, I suppose, but they don't make me feel like…" She trailed off and looked down.

"Like?" he prompted.

"Like myself. I'm not entirely sure who that is, though. I have no idea what 'my style' would be."

"Ah. I understand. Well, how about this—my sister stays over my place sometimes and has a bunch of stuff at my condo. You're welcome to borrow some clothes and whatever else you want."

Once assured that his sister wouldn't mind, Anna accepted the offer. Which meant going to Colt's condo. She'd been in an elevator before, at the hospital. But she'd never gone thirty-two flights up in the sky. She smiled, happy goose bumps popping up on her arms. Everything about working for this man for the next week would be new and incredibly exciting.

As Colt drove past the exit for Grass Creek, Anna's heartbeat felt like it was going faster than his car. She couldn't wait to see where he lived, the tall buildings and crowds and the city lit up at night.

"This is it, up ahead," he said, and she stared up at the huge glass building. He pulled into a garage attached and drove up and around several floors, then parked in a reserved spot. He opened her door and she got out, surrounded by parked cars. Not a buggy in sight.

Colt got the stroller from the trunk and pulled it around to the back passenger-side door, rousing a groggy baby into the stroller. He was gentle, soothing, and said, "Hey, little buddy, we're at my place," then settled the *boppli*—Anna wasn't sure who was who just yet—into the stroller. The baby was fully awake now, the strange surroundings holding his attention. Colt wheeled the stroller to the other side and repeated his actions with his twin, who started to cry.

Anna got out of the car. "I'll take him," she said, scooping up the little one from the car seat. She held him against her chest, gently rocking him, and he quieted.

"A pro. Exactly what I need."

She smiled. "You're pretty good yourself, Colt."

"The novelty hasn't worn off," he said.

Novelty? She supposed that as a single man, an FBI agent living in a big city, he wasn't exactly surrounded by babies. But taking care of others, seeing to their needs, whether a baby or an adult, wasn't something that wore off. She wanted to ask him what he meant, but now the other baby was fussing.

"Noah may be a little jealous," Colt said, glancing at the baby in her arms.

Anna smiled. "I'll bet you're right. And so you must be Nathaniel," she said to the little one she carried. "Let's put you in the stroller next to your twin."

Noah still fussed, so Anna picked him up and rocked him in her arms, letting him stretch a bit. He calmed down, but the moment she tried to put him back in the stroller, he let out a wail. "Okay, little one. My arms, it is."

Colt pushed the stroller with a satisfied Nathaniel, who was biting on his little chew toy.

A couple emerged from an elevator with a little boy, and as the boy ran full speed ahead right toward them, the mother called out, "Don't crash into the nice family!"

Anna froze and she could feel Colt do the same beside her. She recovered first, smiling at the boy who darted past. The couple apologized for their speed demon and moved on.

Colt continued pushing the stroller toward the elevator bank, his entire demeanor...changed. Now he seemed tense. Unsettled. Because of the woman's comment? Because she'd mistaken them for a family? Even in her Amish clothing, her white bonnet, Anna had seemed believable to the woman as the wife of this gorgeous Englisher in his black leather jacket.

Though, with a baby in her arms, and Colt pushing another in the double stroller, they did look like a family. Despite Colt's discomfort, Anna felt a secret thrill at the notion that they were a family. This ridiculously sexy Englisher, her husband. She smiled, the idea so exciting and preposterous that she laughed.

"What did I miss?" he asked, eyeing her as they reached the elevators.

"That woman took us for a family. Can you imagine, an Amish woman, albeit on *rumspringa*, as wife of an FBI agent in Houston?" She couldn't even wonder what that life would be like. When she was little she'd asked her mother if English wives did the same things as Amish wives—the cooking and cleaning and raising of *kinder*, and if they had glamorous jobs or not so glamorous jobs, how they managed everything. Her mother had told her that in the English world, it took a community to help out just the same as in their world. No one could do it all alone.

"This FBI agent can't imagine having *any* wife," Colt said, pushing the button for the elevator.

Her smile faded and she stared at him. He looked dead serious. "You don't plan to marry?"

He shook his head. "I'm fine on my own. I live for my work. In January, I'll be heading up a task force to take down an organized crime ring that's been building in Houston. Getting those thugs off the street and behind bars—that'll take everything I've got. If I had a wife or children, my attention would be split."

She gaped at him. "Split? But your heart would belong to your family completely." Wouldn't it? Jobs were important, of course. Money was necessary to live. But family was the most important thing in this life. Family came first.

The silver elevator doors opened and Colt pushed the stroller inside. Anna stepped next to him, Noah playing with the string of her bonnet.

"I would hope so," he said, running a finger across Noah's big cheek. "But since my heart belongs to my job, I'm sticking with that."

Unsettled, Anna shifted Noah in her arms and pressed her own cheek to his head. She wanted her own family so badly. "Not badly enough that you'll say yes to a *gut* man who loves you," her *aenti* Kate had said more than once. "Not badly enough that you'll commit to being Amish and spending your life as a wife and mother in our village."

She'd even said no to her best friend, Caleb. Handsome. Kind. Loyal. They'd grown up together, but even when she was a girl she didn't dream of marrying Caleb Yoder. She dreamed of what was up the road beyond her sights. She dreamed of hiding in Grass Creek so that the buggies would leave without her. And last year, when Caleb had said he'd waited long enough and had given her an ultimatum, agree to be his wife or he would ask someone else, Anna's heart had broken in two as she'd sobbed that she was sorry but she couldn't marry him.

"If you can't marry Caleb, your best friend, who can you marry?" her *onkel* Eli had asked as he'd dropped off a crib for her to paint. "Who will ever be the right man if not him?"

Those words had gotten inside her and scared her like nothing had. She couldn't say yes to anyone until she knew what life was like outside their village. If she was meant to be Amish. If she was meant to be English. If she was meant to be an Englisher's wife, as she believed deep in her heart.

Maybe not this dashing, 007-type Englisher, who hunted mobsters and vacationed in Macchu Pichu.

Definitely not this Englisher. Who wasn't looking for a wife anyway.

Maybe she would meet her soul mate while in Blue Gulch, and she would know, instantly, that he was the one, that she was meant to be in the English world.

But how could she feel more attraction for any man than she felt for Colt Asher without spontaneously combusting? When she looked at Colt, she felt what she never had when she'd looked at Caleb, who was very good-looking. Who'd sat with her to look up at the stars. Who'd brought her wildflowers. But who didn't really wonder what was beyond their village. He was an Amish man with a wonderful sense of humor and a sparkle in his dark eyes, but he was content. Anna had never been. For the past year, when she ran into

Caleb, he would be polite, but unusually reserved, and make an excuse to walk the other way. He was seriously dating someone now, but still hadn't proposed to her, a fact that made her feel guilty. She wouldn't flatter herself to think he was waiting for her. But part of her did wonder if he was waiting to see what happened, if she would leave and return disappointed, the way her mother had when she'd taken her own *rumspringa* at age sixteen.

Would Anna want to go home at the end of her time away? She really had no idea. How many times had her *aenti* and *onkel* told her she was romanticizing the English world and that a week out there would show her how wonderful and simple life was at home?

You'll know soon enough, she told herself as the elevator doors opened. But so far, every moment of this *rumspringa* felt like Christmas morning.

And in moments she would be inside Colt Asher's home. A whole new world.

Chapter Four

The elevator opened and they emerged into a vestibule. Colt opened a door leading into a pale gray hallway with lovely artwork on the walls. They passed seven doors on both sides, and finally at the end of the hall, Colt stopped to open number 32-8.

Inside his condo, Anna didn't know where to look first—the view of the city out the wall of windows, or the large living room with the stone fireplace, the dark brown leather couches and gorgeous rug and artifacts on the tables and paintings on the walls. On the side of the couch was a big playpen with a few toys inside. Above a couch was a gorgeous framed painting of a world map.

"The guest room is in there," Colt said, pointing to an open door. "In the closet and dresser, you'll find my sister's things. Help yourself."

"Okay on your own with the twins?" she asked.

"I can handle ten minutes," he said, taking off his leather jacket. "Maybe fifteen."

She laughed, but then realized he was serious. *Hmm, perhaps I'll spend this week showing your uncle how to care for* kinder *so that he'll be able to handle a half hour. Or even a whole day. What do you say?* she silently asked adorable Noah as she set him down in the playpen. Colt put his brother beside him, and the two began shaking their brightly colored little toys.

Without his jacket, she could once again see the muscles at work beneath Colt's shirt, how the shirt disappeared into the waistband of his dark gray pants. There were fit Amish men, their muscles honed by construction work, but Anna had never seen anyone as sexy as Colt Asher.

He was staring at her—and she realized it was because she was staring at him. *Eek*, she thought, dragging her gaze away from his amazing body.

"Well, I'll be quick then," she said and disappeared into the room he'd indicated. She was grateful to have a moment alone, to collect herself. She was acting like the love-starved, romance-starved and, yes, let's just put it out there, *sex*-starved woman she was. Oh, God, did Colt Asher know she was a virgin? He must know. But then again, he'd said he didn't know much about Amish culture.

Sex before marriage was against their faith. Once, she and Caleb had come very close, and to be honest, she very likely would have had sex with him but he'd called a halt to things. "If I'm not the one for you, Anna, then don't give yourself to me. I don't want to cause you trouble down the road."

She'd cried at that. That was how much he'd cared about her. But the supposed trouble down the road would only matter in the Amish world, if she chose to marry an Amish man. She didn't tell Caleb that English men didn't expect their wives to be virgins. At least they didn't in the books she'd read. Women had boyfriends and lovers and varying levels of experience. Apparently, it all depended on the woman and how she felt about such matters. An English woman could have a different lover every day or a serious boyfriend or wait until marriage. Anna liked that. She would do what felt right to her. That was all she could go on.

She took a look around the guest room, which was nicely decorated. A bed with a blue-and-white quilt with stars embroidered. A bureau with a mirror, which she also recognized from her village's marketplace in Grass Creek. She opened a drawer. T-shirts and sweaters.

She pulled out a soft cropped-to-the-waist V-necked red sweater and held it up against her in the mirror. There was a thin cotton camisole and she took that, too, then looked in the closet for pants. There was a black jersey wrap dress, a pair of black pants and two pairs of jeans. Luckily, neither was the "skinny" kind that she couldn't imagine being able to breath in.

She took off her dress and put on the camisole, then the sweater, soft and fuzzy against her arms. She put on a pair of jeans, which did not fit like her *daed's* overalls. They weren't too tight but they certainly weren't baggy. Or modest. She zipped up the zipper, something that was forbidden on Amish clothing, and snapped the snap.

She stared at her reflection in the mirror.

Her mouth dropped open.

She looked…like the women she saw in Grass Creek. She looked like an Englisher! The sweater and jeans showed off every curve she didn't really know she had. The Amish didn't have mirrors, which were viewed as promoting vanity, and so Anna only caught her reflection in shop windows in Grass Creek, or in mirrors in the stores she'd explore if there was time on market days. But she'd never seen herself in clothing like this. Clothing that made her feel…sexy.

She took her long hair out of the bun and let it fall.

There was a pair of heels and a pair of sneakers in the closet. Anna took off her boots and tried on both pairs. They fit! Anna kept on the comfortable navy blue sneakers, then once again stood before the mirror. As she stared at herself, a shadow crept where her joy had been.

"I don't know this person," she whispered to her reflection. She bit her lip and turned away. She started to take off the sweater and find something more…Amish. Even a big, button-down shirt would do, but then Anna looked in the mirror again. *For the next week, you are this new person. And sometimes it's not going to feel comfortable. Or familiar. That's okay. That's how you discover what does feel right. That's how you discover who you really are.*

And if after the week it doesn't feel right? You put back on your high-necked dress that goes down to your ankles. You braid your hair and cover your head. And you go home.

She took a deep breath and stepped out, her suitcase now full of his sister's belongings and her own Amish things. Colt was kneeling by the playpen, watching his nephews play. "I think that was just fifteen minutes."

He turned toward her and stood up, staring, his mouth slightly open. "Anna. You're…breathtaking." He glanced down for a moment as though he hadn't meant to say that.

She beamed, so happy, so excited that she didn't even feel herself blush. "I feel like a completely different person."

Dressed this way, she was a person who wanted to rush over to the man who'd just called her breathtaking and kiss him. She had no doubt that one kiss from Colt Asher would rock her entire world and make her knees truly weak, the way she'd read about in books.

He walked toward her and for a moment she wondered if he was going to reach for her and look deeply into her eyes and kiss her. Did that happen in real life? She was sure it did. Was he about to—

He pulled his phone from his pocket and held it up. "My sister also texted the schedule for the babies," he said. "Just in case. So dinnertime is right now. Both boys are on solid foods—jarred baby food."

So much for the hot kiss. The weak knees. Colt Asher was not looking to marry, but she was sure he had relationships. Sex. He would likely not lay a finger on her, though. If she wanted a hot English affair with the FBI agent, she would have to make the first move.

Not that she was ready for that. It was one thing to fantasize. It was another to do it. And she had no idea what she could handle emotionally. Could she have an affair with Colt Asher when it would lead to nothing? Perhaps that was the point of a weeklong, scorching-hot English affair. Wild sex. Then it was over.

Except then what? She wasn't necessarily going home after. Or staying in the English world. She didn't know where she belonged. Until then, she should take care with herself. And her heart. And her body.

It was good that the Englisher was talking about baby food and schedules.

"Do you have groceries?" she asked.

"Of course," he said.

"I thought maybe you were one of those bachelors who didn't cook."

"I have a limited range, but I can certainly open a jar of baby food. And make an omelet and a steak. And pasta. Is there anything else anyway?"

She laughed. "There really isn't. I could eat pasta every day for the rest of my life."

"One day you'll have tortellini in Rome," he said.

She was touched he remembered that from their very first conversation outside her barn, that he'd been listening. "Maybe one day I will."

"What should I make for dinner?" he asked, surprising her. "Given that Noah and Nathaniel are all set with pureed apricots and applesauce and some Toasty O's cereal, I'm thinking I could make my famous western omelets and home fries for us."

"Sounds great," she said with a smile.

While Colt went into the kitchen, which was open-concept and full of stainless steel appliances, Anna watched the babies play. Twenty minutes later, he announced dinner was ready. He even had two baby seats for the dining room table so that the boys could eat with them.

The dining room had another wall of windows and the entire city was lit up. Anna could hardly believe this was her view. She and Colt sat across from each other, a baby next to each of them. Anna fed Noah his apricots; Colt was on applesauce duty with Nathaniel.

"Your nephews are good eaters," she said. "And you're a good cook. Dinner is delicious." He'd surprised her by cooking. By serving dinner. By including the *bopplis* in their conversation instead of pretending they weren't there. Colt Asher would be full of surprises, of that she had no doubt.

Just don't fall in love with the man, she told herself. *You're in lust. You're infatuated. Fine. All good. Just don't get your heart involved or you're in big trouble.*

"According to my sister's schedule, the boys will be ready for bed at seven thirty. Since it's six thirty now and Blue Gulch is a three-hour drive, I'm thinking we should just stay here for the night and start our trip fresh in the morning."

Here. Overnight. Just the two of them? Well, technically there were four of them.

Yes. Yes, yes, yes.

"If you're okay with that," he said. She could tell he was recalling the way her *aenti* and *onkel* had reacted to the thought of her staying in his home.

"I'm perfectly okay with that," she said—too quickly. *Calm down*, she told herself, but she could barely contain her smile.

"The guest-room bed is very comfortable," he added, "and that's per my princess-and-the-pea sister, who complains about four-star hotels' beds. I have a master bath in my bedroom, so the bathroom next to the guest room is all yours. Make yourself at home."

The goose bumps lit up her arms and nape of her neck. She was staying here, in this condo thirty-two

floors up in the Houston sky, overnight with this gorgeous specimen of manhood.

This *rumspringa* could not be off to a more exciting start.

As Colt finished cleaning up after dinner, he could
hear Anna singing softly to the twins in the guest room.
A German lullaby. He was fluent in Spanish and could
understand enough French and Italian to get by, but he
only knew a few German words and phrases. He turned
on the dishwasher and then walked over to the guest
room and peered in. Anna sat in the chair between the
two cribs in the dimly lit room, both twins quiet and
peering at her with droopy eyes.

She continued singing as their eyes closed, and
when she seemed sure they were asleep, she got up
and came out, closing the door behind her.

"Was that an Amish lullaby?" he asked.

"*Ja.* I mean yes. I'm going to try to stick to English
only during my *rumspringa*. But my mother sang me
that lullaby and I always sing it to the babies I tend to.
Puts them right to sleep."

He wanted to reach out and touch her long blond
hair, which curved in front of one shoulder down to
her waist. Her small waist. He thought of the moment
she'd come out of this room earlier in the sweater and
jeans, and it was as if he'd been shot with a cartoon
arrow. He'd gone loopy for a second, unable to breathe
at the sight of her. She'd been beautiful in paint-stained
overalls and a baseball cap. She'd been beautiful in a
loose blue dress to her ankles. She was unbearably sexy
in the little red sweater and tight jeans.

And completely off-limits. Anna might be on her

rumspringa for a week, and she might stay or return to her village and commit to her faith, but either way, he couldn't think of her as available. Even if she was open to it, to experiencing...*him* as part of the English world, a *rumspringa* romance could cause big problems. He had no idea if Anna had ever had a boyfriend, let alone sex, but based on what he knew about the Amish, he doubted it. When the week was up, he would bring his nephews home to their parents and spend the final week of his vacation researching the Duvall crime organization before he brought together the task force to infiltrate the syndicate and gather the necessary evidence to make arrests. Even if Anna decided to become an "Englisher" herself, he wasn't the man for her. He wasn't ever getting married or having children. So he'd be wise to keep his hands off her, no matter how irresistible she was.

"You know what I'd love to do?" she asked.

It could be anything. There were likely so many things she'd never done that he couldn't begin to guess.

She might even say "have mind-blowing sex."

Her pale brown eyes were twinkling. Maybe she *would* say "mind-blowing sex." Maybe she did want to have a no-strings hot romance for a week, after which they'd both walk away.

"Watch my first movie" was what she said. "Something amazing. A classic."

He was equally relieved and disappointed. "A classic. I think we have to go with a Christmas classic. *It's a Wonderful Life*."

"I like the title. Will we have popcorn? That's tradition, right?"

She was way too easy to please. He would have to be very careful around her. Very careful *with* her.

"Popcorn and my favorite beer?" he asked.

"Perfect," she said with a grin.

And so Colt Asher, who'd seen *It's a Wonderful Life* at least five times, found himself watching it again with his nephews' nanny, a big bowl of popcorn on the sofa between them, two beers on the coffee table. Anna was half-covered in a fuzzy orange throw that he'd bought from the Amish market a few months ago. He watched Anna more than he watched the film, which he could probably recite by heart anyway. She smiled and laughed and cried and shook her fist at mean old Mr. Potter.

When the credits rolled, she was wiping away happy tears. "I could watch that every Christmas for the rest of my life."

He smiled. "Wouldn't be Christmas if you didn't."

She turned away and seemed lost in thought.

"Everything okay?" he asked.

"The movie was about realizing what you have. How you've had a big effect even if you hadn't stepped foot from your small town. Clarence the angel would definitely have had a lot to show me. And if there'd been no me, the present would be changed in my village. The future would be changed."

"Has it been a wonderful life?" he asked, sipping his beer.

"Some of it, yes. But it's been a limited life, too."

"Then there's your answer. You can appreciate what you have, what you've had, and still want to experience more. You're not looking to end your life, Anna. You're looking to change it."

She smiled. "I guess you can't really relate. You don't want anything to change. Right?"

He frowned. Was that true? "Except for the criminals off the streets of Houston. Other than that, I'm good." Maybe it *was* true.

"You're lucky to feel content," she said. "That's my goal."

"I didn't say I was content." He took another sip of beer, not really wanting to have this conversation. Talking about himself was one of his least favorite things to do.

A fussy wail came from the guest room. Saved by a seven-month-old. Colt stood. "I'll go see who's up."

She grabbed his hand, sending a little shock wave through him. He was amazed that such a small gesture had such a big impact on his nerve endings. "Wait a few moments. Sometimes a baby will fuss for a few seconds and then soothe himself back to sleep. So you don't want to rush in too soon."

Another fussy wail. Then silence. She was very good at her job.

Well, he could still change the subject.

Colt sat back down and held up his beer glass in a toast. "If you weren't here, I'd have a squawking, tired baby on my lap right now."

She laughed and held her glass up to clink it. "So what did you and my *onk*—my uncle Eli talk about when I went into my house to pack?"

"He asked me to watch out for you. He said you were smart and fearless and deeply curious about the world but that you'd never been farther than Grass Creek for a few hours at a time except for visiting the hospital in Houston and that I should keep that in mind."

She frowned. "It's nice that he cares. But I don't need to be spoken about as if I'm fourteen going on a chaperoned school trip. I'm twenty-four. An adult woman."

Hmm. She'd given him a good idea. If he thought of himself as her chaperone in the English world, he'd erect a glass wall between them so that he could see her but not touch her, not get too close at all. He'd protect her from himself. A man who was incredibly attracted to her but whose intentions would be far from honorable unless honoring her need for wild sex with no strings was the goal. And if it was? Loaded. He'd have to really think about that one.

He shifted slightly over, in the opposite direction so that their knees had no chance of bumping. "Do you think you'll go back after the week is up?"

"It's impossible to say now. So far, I feel very comfortable. I like electricity. I like TV. I like these jeans."

"I do, too," he said, his gaze moving from her long legs to her red sweater and lovely face.

He couldn't take his eyes off her. He found himself memorizing every detail of her pretty face and pale brown eyes, the way one dimple creased in her cheek when she smiled, how her light blond hair frothed over her cheek and down her shoulders to pool at her waist.

She turned toward him and shifted, her curves even more pronounced, and his desire to kiss her was overwhelming. Her lips slightly puckered and she stared at his mouth, then her gaze moved up to his eyes, then back to his mouth. She lightly licked her lips. Was that an invitation? Before he could think or stop himself or even remember his earlier warnings to himself, he leaned closer and closer, giving her the opportunity to frown or lean away or say "Just what do you think you're doing, Englisher?"

But instead she leaned closer, too, lifting up her chin, her pink-red lips so luscious, so close. Their mouths met and he slipped his hands on her face, bringing her even closer. His hands traveled down her neck and explored her back, then slid under the sweater. Unfortunately, she wore a thin shirt underneath when he wanted to feel her skin. He moved his hands to the front of her sweater, needing it off now. But her hands stilled his.

"This may be moving too fast," she said.

It was as if someone snapped fingers in his face and woke him up. He shifted away from her and sat back. Of course it was moving too fast. There should be no movement at all. He shouldn't have kissed her, shouldn't have touched her. He would *not* take advantage of her, no matter how badly he wanted her.

"I think I heard one of the babies," she said and rushed into the guest room.

In a moment she was back. "Colt, since I clearly just contradicted my earlier advice about not racing in to soothe the twins, I just wanted to say I didn't hear anyone. You caught me off guard and I…as the English say, freaked."

He'd freaked, too. At how much he wanted her. How good and right the kiss had felt. "The kiss was a mistake," he said anyway. Because it was true. "It won't happen again."

"I don't think it was a mistake. Or that it shouldn't happen again."

She told it like it was. He liked that. He wished she'd stop being so likable.

"But you're very new to me, Colt Asher. So I'd better say good-night."

"Good night," he said, not wanting her to leave. He wished she'd sit back down and tell him about her village, about her childhood, about her friends and boyfriends—if she'd had any. He wanted to know everything about her.

An arm's length away, though.

Chapter Five

The next day, after a three-hour drive to Blue Gulch, Colt turned onto the main street in the quaint town. Anna peered out the window at the shops and restaurants and small park at the far end, a food truck selling po'boys and cannoli with a line down the block. She felt instantly at home, despite having never been here before. This was a small town, much smaller than Grass Creek, but the bustling downtown was alive with energy and window shoppers and people walking dogs and sitting at the small round tables in front of the bakery, sipping something from small cups with plates of pastry. All the shops were decorated for the holidays, as were some of the trees. Anna smiled as they passed the library, a pizzeria with a guy flipping dough high in the air and a Chinese restaurant, which she would definitely be exploring. A beautiful pink-orange Victorian with a sign that read Hurley's Homestyle Kitchen looked so inviting. She would surely be eating at Hurley's over the next week.

Colt pulled into a small lot just a couple of doors down from the restaurant. The Blue Gulch Inn. Like Hurley's, the inn was a Victorian. It was a pretty shade of yellow with a white door and a white picket fence. This was to be home for the next week. Colt checked them in, and then they headed back to his SUV to bring in all the baby paraphernalia, the portable cribs and playpen and the twins' toys.

As passersby smiled, particularly as Colt set each twin in the stroller, once again Anna loved being mistaken for the mother, the twins her children, the gorgeous FBI agent her husband. Last night, this morning, now—everything seemed like a dream, like one of her fantasies, but she was really here, dressed in these clothes, her life completely different than it had been yesterday morning. *This* morning she'd woken up in Colt's guest room surprised that she knew exactly where she was, that she was taking care of twin babies and not three calves. *Because this feels right and strangely comfortable*, she thought. The babies had each woken up once during the night, but Anna had hardly slept anyway, her mind on the man down the hall. She wondered if he was thinking about her and their kiss. If he wanted more, much more. She'd wondered if he slept naked the way a friend had told her all Englishers did.

Her first night as an almost Englisher, *she* hadn't slept naked. For one thing, she needed to pop out of bed to care for the babies. For another, if Colt knocked on her door and she was naked, after having spent hours thinking about his gorgeous face and rock-hard body, who knew what urges would overcome her. She might "jump his bones." Considering that she'd called a halt to their kiss, which had led to traveling hands, she doubted she'd do anything. But she did know it wasn't wise to rush into sex with a man who made her feel things she'd never felt.

"Our rooms are on the first floor for ease with the babies," he said as they followed the proprietor down the hall. The inn was lovely, full of antiques and vases of flowers and interesting paintings and rugs.

Their rooms were at the back of the house, right across from each other. After helping them carry in the babies' things to Anna's room, the owner gave them their keys, let them know breakfast was between seven and eight thirty and then left them alone.

To accommodate the porta-cribs and equipment, Colt had booked Anna the largest room, and she loved the French doors that led into a private fenced yard.

"What a beautiful room," she said, looking all around as Colt stood in the doorway, his hand on the twins' stroller. The room had a seaside theme. There were big shells on the bureau, which had a huge round mirror, and a rose-colored quilt decorated with tiny starfish. There was a rocking chair in a corner, perfect for calming the *bopplis* to sleep.

He smiled. "Why don't we head next door to Hurley's?" he asked. "In one of our emails, my twin told me it's a favorite in Blue Gulch. Best barbecue in the county."

She loved this life. Small-town inns. Barbecue. And Colt. For an entire week. "Sounds good," she said.

A few minutes later, Colt pushed the stroller down

the sidewalk toward the restaurant, and since there were three big steps leading up to a porch, they parked the stroller out of the way and each took a baby.

"What cuties!" a waitress said, ogling Noah and Nathaniel. "We have baby seats for the tables. It'll be about ten minutes, though."

Since it was just past noon, the restaurant was crowded, but there were only two groups ahead of them in line. They stood, each holding a baby, Anna bouncing Noah a bit and pointing out all the pretty colors on the porch, Colt playing peekaboo with Nathaniel with one hand.

She loved watching him like this. He seemed to think he wasn't this kind of guy, but he was in unguarded moments.

Suddenly, Anna heard a woman gasp, and she and Colt both glanced up.

A redhead, in her late forties Anna guessed, stared at Colt, her mouth open, her green eyes misty with tears. "Are you...?" she began, then paused, taking a step back. The man beside her put his arm protectively around hers. "Are you Colt Asher? I mean, of course you are. You're Colt Asher."

"I am," he said. "I suppose you know that because I look a lot like my twin, Jake."

The woman pressed her lips together and brought her hand up to cover her mouth. She composed herself, then said, "I'm Sarah Mack Ford." She waited a beat to see if the name meant anything to him.

It clearly did. Colt's eyes widened for a moment, then he, too, composed himself, and Anna could tell he wasn't used to be being caught off guard. "You're my birth mother," he whispered.

Sarah nodded. "Jake told me you would be back sometime in November or December. I know you two only had a brief visit back in May. I hope we can spend some time together while you're here. This is my husband, Edmund Ford."

Colt shook hands with Edmund, a distinguished-looking man in his fifties.

"I'd throw my arms around you in a hug," Sarah said, her eyes misting again, "but I don't want to smush the sweet baby you're holding. I didn't know you had children," she said, smiling at Anna and the baby in her arms.

"These rascals are my nephews," Colt explained. "And Anna—Anna Miller—is the nanny I hired to help me out for the week I'm on babysitting duty. My sister and her husband had a sitter snafu and a cruise booked, so uncle to the rescue. Anna to the rescue, I should say."

Anna shook hands with the couple. For a moment she waited for the barrage of questions that she often got in Grass Creek while tending the Amish market. *Do Amish people really not use electricity? Have you ever used a cell phone? Do you have outhouses?* Then she remembered she was dressed as an Englisher. Wasn't wearing a bonnet. And her insanely long hair was up in a ponytail. She looked like everyone else in the restaurant.

"Are you staying in town?" Edmund asked Colt. "You're welcome to stay with us."

"We're at the Blue Gulch Inn," Colt said. "But thank you. I don't think you want to be woken up by not one but two babies all night long."

Edmund smiled. "I did just get past that stage with

my grandson, Danny. He's two and a half and sleeping like a champ these days."

"Your table is ready," the waitress said, smiling at Colt and Anna. "Right this way."

"Perhaps you can come for dinner tonight or tomorrow night?" Sarah asked. "I'll invite Jake, as well."

"Tonight works for me," Colt said. Anna watched him take in the woman, the way he had when he'd first come to her village. He was studying his birth mother's features, her hair, her height, her mannerisms. She wondered if he was looking for himself in his biological mother.

They exchanged cell phone numbers and then the couple headed down the porch steps while the waitress led Colt and Anna to their table. Many friendly diners smiled and waved at the twins. This town sure was welcoming.

Once they were seated, Noah and Nathaniel in their baby seats with their beloved Cheerios and favorite pureed baby food on their trays, Anna studied the menu. Blackened chicken po'boy with a side of spicy sweet potato fries—yes, please. Colt also ordered a po'boy, his pulled pork with the house barbecue sauce and a side of coleslaw.

"Wow," Anna said once the waitress left. "You just met your birth mother. For the first time."

Colt only nodded, and then saved a Cheerio from being shot off the table by Noah. He turned his attention to Nathaniel, who was staring at a little boy at the next table. "That'll be you in a few years," Colt said, smiling. "Whoops," he added, turning to Noah. "Maybe we'll save these Cheerios for later. I think we have a hockey great in our presence." He moved the Cheerios out of sliding range.

Huh. Colt had completely avoided her comment. Avoided further discussion. She wondered what that was about. He seemed so…nonchalant. He'd just met his biological mother. A woman who recognized him, albeit because he had a twin who looked a lot like him, but still, she knew him the moment she saw him. That had to mean something to Colt.

"Have you always wanted to find your birth mother?" she asked.

"No," he said. "My sister was always curious about her biological family and began searching at eighteen. She was very disappointed at what she found. Anyway, my parents were my parents and that was all I needed to know."

That didn't sound like an FBI agent. Colt struck her as the kind of man who'd turn over every stone for the smallest detail. But his biological family and his thoughts on the matter were not her business.

The waitress brought over their drinks, homemade lemonade in small mason jars, and Colt seemed grateful for the break in conversation. He'd planned on visiting his twin and meeting his birth mother, so he certainly wasn't closed to the idea. But Anna could tell he had a wall up, and so she wouldn't pry.

After forty-five minutes in Hurley's, Colt had to get out of there. He had no idea that so many people would come to him and say, "You must be related to Jake Morrow. You look just like him!" At least ten had.

Before he'd even finished his po'boy he'd gotten a text from Jake himself. Heard through the grapevine that you're in town. Glad you're here. Let me know when we can get together. Then five minutes later, another. Sarah just called—see you tonight at her house at six thirty.

Small towns were like this. Half of him liked the idea of people knowing another, checking in, having community. But the other half was more comfortable in Houston, where he would walk down the street anonymously. Where he wouldn't run into anyone. Where he'd decide where and when to meet someone. Where he could prep. Colt believed in prep. *Never walk in cold* was another of his many mottos.

His birth mother had rattled him. There'd been no prep. He should have assumed he'd run into her in a town as small as Blue Gulch. He also should have assumed that, given how alike he and Jake looked, people would comment. He'd wanted to meet Sarah Mack on his terms, when he was ready. Then again, sometimes, there was no ready. It wasn't as if he could possibly know how he'd feel when he met his birth mother. So what was there to prepare for? He'd done a basic background check on her and had seen a photograph, so the sight of her hadn't been a complete surprise. They— she, Jake and he—all had the same green eyes. She was tall, too. He'd planned on setting up a get-together with Sarah while he was in town, but had figured he'd get to know his twin a bit first before meeting his birth mother. Colt had never liked not knowing what to expect, so maybe it really was better that they'd run into each other. The notion of meeting her wasn't going to gnaw at his gut. It was done.

Finally, the plates were cleared and Colt settled the

bill, politely smiled through a few rounds of "your babies are so adorable! You are so blessed!"

He and Anna had stopped correcting people a half hour ago. At first, he would explain that they were his nephews, and Anna would mention that she was the nanny. But after a while, they realized they'd never get through their po'boys if they didn't stop talking, so they just smiled.

Each carrying a twin, they headed down the porch steps toward the inn.

"Aww, your twins are so cute!" a woman said.

He smiled and nodded. "It's amazing to me that so many people could mistake me for a father," he whispered to Anna. "I'm the least dad-ish guy there is."

"Well, either you have everyone fooled or..."

He glanced at her. "Or what?"

"Or you seem dad-ish to people. You dote on the twins. You look at them with love in your eyes. Dad-ish."

"You mean uncle-ish," he said. Definitely uncle-ish.

She had a sly smile on her pretty face. "I suppose." As they reached the inn and headed inside, she added, "Well, I'll get the boys settled for their naps."

It was clear from her expression that she knew he needed some time to himself. He liked that she could read him, and he knew he wasn't an easy guy to read.

Except Noah started screaming his little head off as they walked down the hall to their rooms.

Anna tried rocking him in her arms. Didn't help. Gave him a good burp. Didn't help. Sang him a song he'd loved on the ride to Blue Gulch this morning.

"Waaaahhh!" Noah screeched.

"Before the entire inn hates us, I'll get him in the room," she said.

He followed her into the room. "What do you think is bothering him?"

Anna peered at Noah. His face seemed a bit red to Colt, but maybe because he was screeching. "Maybe gas. Let's try some bicycling."

"Babies can ride bikes?"

She raised an eyebrow and brought Noah over to her bed and laid him on his back. He continued to squawk. Then she raised up his legs and began to pump each in a pedaling motion.

"Ah," Colt said. "Biking with no bike."

"Sometimes it works to propel gas from the tummy." She continued to pedal Noah's legs and soon enough, the crying stopped. He flipped over onto his stomach and then sat up, his eyes drooping. "Let's get you down for your nap, sleepyhead." She scooped up the baby and changed his diaper, then settled him down in the crib. He fussed a bit, and she sang to him until he quieted.

Colt felt guilty just standing around while she did all the heavy lifting, even if she was the twins' nanny. He took Nathaniel over to the changing table and set him down, unsnapped his little bodysuit and untaped his bulky diaper. "Ooh, that couldn't have been too comfortable," he said. He turned to Anna. "Uh, do I put baby powder on him?"

"You can keep him exposed to the air for a minute or two, then sprinkle some powder on him."

"Don't pee on me," he said to Nathaniel. "That wouldn't be nice to do to Uncle Colt."

Anna laughed. "I've been peed on a time or two."

He sprinkled the powder and managed to get a fresh diaper on the baby. "That wasn't so hard."

Anna was looking at Nathaniel in Colt's arms. "They're lucky. *You're* lucky. I always wanted a sibling. They have each other, twin brothers. You have a sister and now these beautiful nephews growing your family. Plus you have a twin of your own."

"I've always been something of a lone wolf," he said. "I mean, I'd do anything for my sister. Obviously. But before the twins were born, I rarely saw her. Maybe every few months for a quick check-in call, and I'd see her on holidays that she insisted on making a fuss over."

Anna reached for Nathaniel, and Colt handed him over. "And since your nephews were born, you get together more often?"

He watched Anna lay down the baby in his crib. "At least once a month. I make it a priority. If I know I'll be away on a case, I'll try to get more time in before I go."

Anna turned on the lullaby player. For a moment they watched the babies' little mouths twitch, their heavy eyelids lower and raise, then lower. Maybe he wasn't as much as a lone wolf as he thought. The birth of the twins had meant something to him; the family connection, the promise of a future generation meant something to him. Otherwise, he would have continued on as always.

"But family must be important to you, Colt. You're also here in Blue Gulch right now. However you and your twin came together, you were part of that."

"I suppose. As I said, I didn't even know I had a twin until this past May. I received an email at my work account from a guy named CJ Morrow. He said he and his brother—my twin—found my name among some papers in his father's old trunk and that Jake had wanted to meet me since he discovered I existed five years ago, but that CJ had been uncomfortable with it. Apparently, CJ still didn't like the idea of his big bro having a twin out there, but CJ didn't think it was fair to let his insecurity stand in the way of Jake meeting me."

"Wow, that was generous of Jake's brother. Sounds like it wasn't easy for him to write that email, let alone mail it."

He smiled. "You mean 'hit Send.'"

"Hit Send," she repeated with a grin. "Got it."

"I thought so, too. I found myself undercover a couple towns away on a gunrunning case, so I just stopped by Jake's ranch. I don't know what I was thinking. I'm not the drop-in type."

"Sometimes, when dealing with something new and the brain hasn't caught up to the heart, one acts first, thinks later. Sometimes that's good. In this case, it sure was."

"I think so. Otherwise, I might have just emailed CJ back a couple lines about how I was busy on a case and let it go. But something *did* make me respond— in person. Suddenly, standing right in front of me was my twin brother. We were both pretty blown away by the sight of each other."

"I'll bet. What's he like?"

"Seems like a good guy. He married a woman— Emma—who was pregnant when she began working at his ranch as the cook. Now, they're very happily married with a newborn. We've emailed a bit over the past several months. But I said I'd come back in November or December when my case was finished. So here I am." He smiled, watching the twins sleep. "I did think I'd have a week to myself between that rough case and coming here, but that wasn't to be, thanks to these little scamps."

"Life is like that."

"Sure is," he said.

"Maybe one day I'll be lucky and find my cousin," Anna said. "It's nerve-racking leaving home and I'm twenty-four. Mara was only seventeen when she left. And that was twenty-five years ago. I don't even know if she's still in Texas."

"I can do some poking around if you'd like," Colt said.

Her eyes lit up. "It's good to know an FBI agent."

"Unless you're a bad guy."

She laughed and Noah stirred, so she put a finger to her lips. Lips he'd kissed the night before and hadn't stopped thinking about.

He'd tossed and turned on his very comfortable bed, remembering how she'd driven him wild by just sitting there beside him, looking beautiful and sexy. A not-family guy who'd be checking out very soon to devote himself 24/7 to the organized-crime-syndicate case? Not for Anna Miller. She'd been wise to stop him before things could get out of hand. And try as he had last night to *not* fantasize about her and what they'd do in this bed, he couldn't get her off his mind.

And now she was all "up in his business," to use a favorite phrase of perps. She knew about his twin. She'd met his birth mother when he had, for God's sake. She'd been in his condo, stayed the night there.

He rarely brought women home, wanting to keep his place his sanctuary.

A text pinged on his phone. Would love for you to bring Anna and the twins to dinner. Jake and Emma will bring their baby. See you at 6:30. 100 Thornton Lane.

Talk about a family affair. Anna was getting more and more enmeshed in his life. He didn't like it. But he needed her round-the-clock for the babies.

"My birth mother extended the invitation to you and the babies for dinner tonight. If you'd like to come," he whispered, glancing at his napping nephews. "Jake's wife and their baby are coming, too."

Maybe she'd be happy to stay at the inn or wheel the babies around Blue Gulch. Why would she want to come to his awkward not-family dinner?

But she beamed. "I'd love to!"

And he wasn't sure how he felt about walking into a room full of his biological family all at once. Granted, he'd already met Jake, albeit for five minutes back in May. And he'd met Sarah and her husband for two minutes this afternoon. He would have preferred spending time with each one-on-one, easing into this new territory.

He didn't like new territory, aka emotions that he'd never experienced before. Colt liked to know what to expect. No surprises.

Now he was going to have dinner with two couples who were a fundamental part of him, his past, his history. How could there not be surprises?

Chapter Six

"Whoa. Your birth mother lives here?" Anna asked as they arrived at 100 Thornton Lane.

Was this even a house? Made of stone, the three-story building looked like a castle. The grounds were beautiful with a huge front yard and a gorgeous barn, the traditional red, and a pasture, which indicated there were horses.

Anna glanced down at her outfit. She'd changed from jeans into Colt's sister's black pants and had paired it with a beaded silver sweater and pretty suede boots with heels. At first she'd been worried she'd be overdressed; now she was glad she'd spiffed up.

Colt parked next to a silver pickup, and they each scooped up a baby from the car seats and headed to the stately front door.

Anna wondered if a butler would answer. One did!

A man in a uniform like a tuxedo smiled and opened the door. "Good evening. My name is Lars. May I have your names?"

"Colt Asher and Anna Miller," Colt said, one eyebrow raised.

"And Noah and Nathaniel," Anna added, shifting the baby in her arms.

The butler nodded and smiled at the babies, then resumed his stiff posture. "Very good. Please follow me to the library."

The library. How fancy! Anna had never been in a mansion. And had never followed a butler.

The butler opened French doors and said, "Mr. Colt Asher and Ms. Anna Miller, plus masters Noah and Nathaniel."

"Lars, no need to be so formal," Sarah Mack Ford said with a smile as she rushed over. She took Colt's hand in both of hers, then did the same to Anna. "Welcome to our home. We have the family room all set up for the babies to crawl around. Lars's wife, Leanna, our cook and housekeeper, has asked to be on babysitting duty while we eat. She misses babies."

A butler and a housekeeper. Such things didn't exist back home. You cleaned your house yourself. You cooked your own meals. If a friend or neighbor fell ill, you cooked and cleaned for them, as well.

Edmund greeted them, as well, and after a few minutes of conversation, Sarah and Edmund led the way to the family room, where a couple sat close together on a sofa. The man, who looked remarkably like Colt, was holding an infant in his arms.

"Jake and Emma," Sarah said, "Colt and Anna are here with Colt's baby nephews."

After so many people remarked earlier that Colt must be related to Jake Morrow, Anna could now see why there was no mistaking the relation. Colt and his twin looked almost identical, but Colt's features were more intense, more angular. Both had the same thick dark hair and green eyes. Both were tall and muscular.

The couple stood and walked over. Jake carefully gave his wife the baby, and then extended his hand to Colt. "I'm glad you're here. I've been looking forward to this for months."

"I wasn't planning on bringing company," Colt said, grinning at the baby in his arms and gesturing at the other in Anna's. "But my sister's sitter had to cancel right before she and her husband were leaving for a weeklong cruise. So I stepped in."

"They're beautiful," Emma said. "I'm so glad to meet you, Jake. And you, Anna. This is our baby daughter, Violet."

Anna peered over at the breathtaking infant, her eyes closed, silky blond wisps on her head. Between the twins and Violet, Anna was socked with an overpowering desire for her own baby, a baby to raise, love, cherish. Her arms suddenly ached just as her aunt always said would accompany the feeling. When Anna would try to explain to *Aenti* Kate that she couldn't marry this man or that because she didn't feel enough, Kate would say that one day, Anna's arms would ache for a baby and perhaps then she'd be ready to accept a proposal. But Anna knew it wasn't wanting a baby that would lead her to marry. It was the particular man who'd make her happy to say yes. And then her arms would ache.

She froze, wondering what this meant. Maybe her

fantasies about Colt Asher had gone a tad too far. When his sister and brother-in-law returned from the cruise, Colt would bury himself in research on the new case, then be off in the field. And yes, he might be attracted to her, but that didn't mean it went any deeper. She'd have to be more careful about her feelings for Colt. But *could* you be careful with your feelings?

As Jake and Edmund made a fuss over Noah and Nathaniel, and Anna chatted with Emma—it turned out they both grew up on farms, though Emma's was strictly crops—she noticed Colt going outside into the backyard with his birth mother and they began walking along the manicured path. She could see by the set of his shoulders, the tightness in his face, that he wasn't exactly comfortable, though his expression was perfectly pleasant. He was trying very hard, she supposed. But Anna sensed that Colt was counting down the days until his sister returned and he could go off on his own.

Over dinner, which was perfectly cooked steaks, roasted potatoes and asparagus, Colt listened to the crazy story of how Sarah and her husband had found each other. A fortune-teller had told widowed Edmund Ford that his second great love was a hairstylist named Sarah with green eyes. Edmund's son, Carson, a private investigator, insisted on finding the woman for his starry-eyed father, but only to prove that the fortune was a scam and a lie. But the green-eyed hairstylist had proved difficult to find until Carson got the fortune-teller's daughter, Olivia, involved. The mystery woman turned out to be Olivia's estranged aunt, Sarah. And one fortune had brought together an aunt and a niece and two couples—Sarah and Edmund, and Carson and Olivia.

"How romantic!" Anna said. "And it gives me hope. My cousin Mara estranged herself from my family years ago and I'm hoping to find her while—while I'm in a different part of Texas."

"I was estranged from my niece Olivia for five years," Sarah said. "And I hated every moment of it. I do hope you find your cousin. I'm sure Colt can help. And Edmund's son, Carson, the private investigator, can help, too."

"What if she doesn't want to be found, though?" Anna asked, putting her fork down.

"I didn't want to be found," Sarah said. "Until I was. And then it was the happiest day of my life. Finding me brought a lot of people together. So you go get that cousin of yours."

Colt watched Anna's face brighten. If it was the last thing he did, he'd reunite her with her cousin. It would be a good Christmas present.

"This entire table is about family being brought together," Jake said. "In many different ways." He put his hand on his wife's, and she beamed up at him.

Colt glanced at his twin. He liked the guy, liked his wife. But he wasn't all that sure he belonged here. Would there be another dinner, another get-together? For what purpose? Colt was fine with meeting Jake Morrow—especially after that heartfelt email he'd received from Jake's younger brother. And Colt was relieved he'd finally met his birth mother, who seemed like a lovely person, as was her husband. But Colt wasn't interested in getting to know these people better. He had a family—his sister. His nephews. He wasn't looking to add to his family. These people were part of him, sure, but now that he'd met them, spent a little time with them, he was ready to move on. He was sure they'd understand. They were really just strangers, though Jake and Sarah seemed to have developed a nice relationship.

As dinner ended, everyone got up to clear the table since the butler and housekeeper had made a quiet dinner possible by babysitting in the family room.

"Men clearing the table," Anna said, her driftwood-colored eyes wide. "Of all the new things I've experienced, I'll never get over the novelty of watching a man stack dirty plates and carry them into the kitchen."

Everyone froze and gaped at Anna.

"Come from a very traditional family?" Emma asked, eyebrow raised.

Anna bit her lip, and Colt realized she'd just given herself away. He knew she wanted to pass as an Englisher.

"Very," Anna said. "I'm Amish. Colt and I met while he was on business in my village and we chatted a bit about how I never got the chance to take my *rumspringa*, when Amish teens experience life in the English world. Since I have experience babysitting and he needed a nanny, he hired me for the week. I'm seeing a lot of things for the first time."

"Edmund and I drove down to Grass Creek to shop in the Amish market for a baby crib for Violet," Sarah said. "Are you from the Amish community near there?"

Anna picked up two empty platters from the table. "Yes. I spent quite a lot of time at the market at my family's stall. I paint the furniture my family builds."

"What happens after a *rumspringa*?" Jake asked,

leading the way across the hall into the large kitchen with a stack of plates in his hands. "Do some Amish people prefer life outside the community and choose not to return?"

Anna set the platter down on the counter. "Yes. But it's rare. Especially in my village."

"So your cousin—she chose not to return?" Emma asked, opening the dishwasher.

"Actually, as far I know, she wasn't even interested in having a *rumspringa*. Something happened and she left. There were lots of rumors—that she got pregnant and was ashamed, so she fled. Or that she fell madly in love with an Englisher and just never looked back. But to just up and leave your family and never look back? It's been almost twenty-five years."

Colt reached for Anna's hand and gave it a gentle squeeze. "Between Edmund's son and me, we'll get you two reunited. You can count on it."

Anna's worried expression faded. "Thank you, Colt. That means a lot."

"Check on the babies?" Jake asked Colt, and the two headed into the family room while everyone else got the coffee and tea going and started bringing out dessert to the dining room.

In the huge family room, Colt's nephews were crawling around inside a big fenced area, full of foam blocks and musical toys. Leanna was sitting on a rocker, baby Violet fast asleep in her arms while her husband, Lars, sat near the play area, encouraging a baby crawl race.

"Thanks for watching the boys," Colt said. "We'll take over. Go on and have a drink and some of that delicious pie I saw in the kitchen."

"Don't mind if I do," Lars said.

Leanna stood, carefully transferring Violet to Jake, who cradled the baby girl in his arms.

As Lars and Leanna left, Jake walked over to where Colt stood, watching his nephews. "She feels like my own flesh and blood," Jake said. "Sometimes I forget she's not my biological daughter."

Colt looked at the sleeping newborn in Jake's arms. "She's a lucky one to have you as a father, then."

Jake smiled. "Thanks for coming tonight. I know you said you'd come back but I wasn't really sure you would. I don't know why I got that impression."

"Maybe because I knocked on your door back in May and only stayed for five minutes," Colt said. "I guess I'm not sure how to feel about any of this. Suddenly having family ties I didn't have six months ago. Meaning you—of course, I knew I had a birth mother. I had no intention of finding her, though."

"No curiosity?" Jake asked. "I had a great childhood, terrific parents. But I always wondered about my biological mother and father, what they looked like, what my story was, what *their* story was."

"I never thought much about it. My parents were a bit on the distant side. They took good care of us, my sister and me, but I guess I was always too busy chasing after my father's respect to wonder about parents who I never knew."

"Is your dad also in law enforcement?" Jake asked.

"He was FBI also. A thug after payback stalked him and my mother as they were heading out to dinner one night. I was twenty-two, my sister twenty." Why the hell was he saying any of this? He hadn't meant to talk about that. Colt could feel Jake's eyes on him.

"I'm very sorry," his twin said.

"I never talk about it. I'm not sure why I did just now. Way to kill the mood, huh?"

"I'm just glad to know you, Colt," Jake said. "I'd much rather skip the surface and small talk and go straight to the real stuff."

Colt nodded. His twin was great. But he wanted—needed—to get the hell out of here, where the walls, despite being mansion-feet away, were closing in on him. Maybe this was just too much, all at once. His birth mother. His twin. Sharing the hardest time of his life when he'd kept that night, his parents' anniversary, bottled up. He and his sister lit two candles every February 9 and shared a moment—hell, an hour, at least—of silence every year, but they rarely spoke of that night.

"Dessert's on," Leanna said, coming back into the family room. "You two go fill up on pie and cake and coffee. I'll watch the three little ones."

Jake pressed a kiss to his daughter's forehead and stared down at her, the tenderness on his face something to behold. Colt could tell Jake didn't really want to give up the infant in his arms. From his expression, his body language, the look in Jake's eyes, Colt could see the man felt very much at home with fatherhood.

Colt couldn't imagine ever feeling that way.

Chapter Seven

"Well," Colt said, "we'd better get these little guys home to bed."

Anna glanced up from where she sat on the family room floor with Noah and Nathaniel, the boys banging on a soft piano toy that Edmund had said was a favorite of his two-year-old-nephew, Danny. She didn't want to leave. Though part of her wanted to have some time with Colt, another part could stay here forever, listening to these people talk about their lives and what was going on in the world and who they ran into yesterday and where to get the best pizza in Blue Gulch. The conversation moved at a slightly dizzying pace, and Anna loved every minute. Get-togethers in her village focused on which families could use a little help, which pieces of furniture sold the best at the market and what new ones they might try, and anything that might need addressing by the bishop at the next church service. From naughty children to those who weren't pulling their weight, the bishop would work the gist of the issue into his sermon and that usually took care of that.

She'd lived in the English world for twenty-four hours and already felt at home here. Her heart had always been leading her outside of her community, so it wasn't a surprise. But then again, she'd been here one day. A week from now, maybe she'd discover she'd had enough, that simple and plain were something to treasure, that life without electricity and cell phones and zippers and beaded sweaters was just fine. She was also cocooned right now, she knew. She had a job. A very tall, strong law-enforcement officer for a boss, by her side 24/7. A lovely room at an inn. Being on her own would be quite different.

Anna got up and handed a twin to Colt before picking up the other. "Sarah, at dinner you mentioned that you're a hairstylist. Do you work in a salon?"

Sarah nodded. "I opened my own salon right here in town."

"I'd love to get my hair cut," Anna said, touching the bun she'd wrapped her waist-length hair into.

"I have a full day tomorrow but I'd be happy to take care of you before I open. Can you be at the salon at nine? It's called Hair by Sarah and it's just about a half mile down from where we met at lunch today. Next to the bookstore."

Anna bit her lip. She couldn't just leave the twins for an hour while she pampered herself. Perhaps Sarah would come to the inn and cut her hair in her room? Or was that crazy to ask? She was about to suggest it.

"I'll watch the twins while you're gone," Colt said.

Anna was touched. "Thank you, Colt. If they wake at five the way they did this morning, they may be ready for their nap at nine, so that'll work out great."

"If they're awake and raring to play," Jake said, "bring them over to the ranch."

"I might just do that," Colt said with a nod.

Anna turned to Sarah. "Well, then, Sarah, I'll definitely see you tomorrow at nine." Yes! She was finally getting her hair professionally cut.

The group walked Colt and Anna to the door and said their goodbyes, and they headed back to the car.

"I had a wonderful time," Anna said. "They're lovely people."

"They do seem to be."

Anna glanced at him as he loaded Noah in his car seat. "Seem? As in they might not be?"

"Well, it's the second time I met either of them," Colt said. "So 'seem' seems appropriate."

She frowned and walked around to the other side of the car to settle Nathaniel in his seat. "Is it your job that forces you to be distrusting?"

He looked at her as though she had five heads. "Well, I am in the bad-guy business. But *life* has made me distrusting, Anna. Nothing wrong with erring on the side of caution in all things."

"You hired me as your baby twin nephews' nanny after knowing me for all of ten minutes."

"Touché," he said. "But I made up my mind about you."

"In ten minutes?"

"Yes. I saw how you responded to me when I first approached. Did you pretend you didn't know a girl with red pigtails? Did you try to get me to leave? Or did you lead me right to the pint-sized perpetrator? And did you make your cousin get in huge trouble with her parents? Or did you teach her that sometimes kids make mistakes and a valuable lesson can be found in understanding motivation and acting accordingly?"

"I suppose it *was* a packed ten minutes," she said.

He smiled. "I listen, Anna. Closely. The way you handled Sadie. The conversation we had afterward. My gut told me you were kind and trustworthy. That and the fact that you were looking for a way to experience your *rumspringa*, and I knew we could help each other out."

"But didn't the entire evening we just spent with Sarah and Jake tell you what you needed to know about them? They're both wonderful."

"I'm not hiring them to be my nanny for a week, though," Colt said.

"Meaning you're okay with temporary relationships only?"

"I told you, Anna. I'm a lone wolf. I work alone—with backup as needed, but alone. I live alone. I'm not looking to fill my world with people." He opened the passenger door for her and she slid into the seat.

She gaped at him, unable to understand how he could feel the way he did. "I am." She buckled her seat belt, grateful for the feeling of being tethered to something at the moment.

"We're very different," he said as he shut the door.

"Then why do you feel like a kindred spirit?" she whispered and then hoped she hadn't said it aloud. But dang it, she had.

If he'd heard her, he didn't say anything. He'd closed

her car door just as the words had tumbled out of her mouth.

Unsettled, she turned toward the window and peered out at the night, the lights inside the welcoming mansion breaking the darkness.

Don't you fall in love with this man, she warned herself.

But as he got inside the driver's side, she was aware, again, of how close he was, how gorgeous his strong profile was, the way his hand rested on the steering wheel. And suddenly she was remembering their kiss, the one he'd said was a mistake and shouldn't happen again, and she knew she was halfway in love with him already.

The English fall in and out of love all the time, some of her Amish friends had told her after their *rumspringas*. Anna recalled the way Sarah and Edmund and Emma and Jake had looked at each other during the evening. Their love for one another glowed in their faces, in their eyes. If it wasn't greedy to have two Christmas wishes, Anna would ask not just to find her cousin, but to experience that kind of love for herself. To look at a man that way. To have him look at her that way.

Anna couldn't imagine feeling for another man what she felt for Colt Asher.

Sharp left, jab to the right. One, two. Knockout! He's down for the count!

Colt still hadn't really gotten up. Or recovered from Anna's comment. *A kindred spirit.* Colt was an Amish woman's kindred spirit? Women had accused him of all sorts of things over in the past, since he'd first noticed Laurel Cuthman in eighth grade science class.

He'd been so attracted to her that he couldn't concentrate in any class, not just science. And thinking of her came unbidden whether he tried to clear his mind or not. He'd gotten better at that over the years, and now could be like a Jedi if he wanted. If he *had* to be. But Laurel had accused him of not really liking her, just wanting her for her body, and he hadn't understood the difference. Her body *was* her, he'd explained, and he'd gotten a poke in the chest and a frown and a "come back when you care what my favorite food is, or flower, or if I have a good relationship with my older sister."

The thing is, he had cared about all that, but he didn't want to talk about those things with Laurel or with anyone. When he was with a girl as a teenager, he only wanted to disappear from his house, from his father's disapproval. Kissing, touching, that was what he wanted. And with each girl and woman that was okay until it wasn't, until they demanded more in the forms of ultimatums. Colt always went his own way, looking for his own kindred spirit—a woman who'd let him be.

He thought he'd found her in Jocelyn Akers, a woman who was everything he wanted. She seemed to instinctively know when he needed to be by himself, or when he needed quiet, or when he needed her to come over and just be with him after a difficult day. She'd been the perfect woman for just over a month until he discovered she was a very high-level drug dealer hoping an FBI-agent boyfriend would look the other way if and when he uncovered her secret life. He hadn't looked the other way—of course not—and set up a sting that got her and several of her associates arrested. How could he not have known? The great Colt

Asher had been tricked, fooled, bamboozled. His faith in people had taken a serious nosedive.

The experience had made him aware that he was all too human and had to work on that, and it wasn't all that hard, given how angry he was at being conned, to steel up his insides. Not much got through. There was room for his sister and his nephews. That was it.

He wasn't Anna Miller's kindred spirit. How she could think he was, though, made him wonder what she saw in him that he wasn't putting out there. Colt was a believer in control, and he thought he was in firm control of himself. So what could possibly make her think he was anything like her? She was sweet, kind, loving, joyful, curious about the world and truly brave. She'd left behind everything she knew to discover who she was and how she felt, to follow her heart. That was courage. Especially because she was so damn unshielded, unprotected. He ran headfirst into dangerous situations for a living, but he had a gun. Backup. Weeks of research on what he was stepping into. Anna was just going merrily along, letting herself experience this new life. And she might not like everything she saw and felt.

He wasn't her kindred spirit and he had to make sure she knew that. If she was pinning any kind of hope on him, she'd end up with a broken heart and he would not allow himself to be the reason she returned to her village.

He'd take a big step back. He'd act like her boss. Their relationship from now on would be strictly professional.

When he got home, he'd kiss his nephews goodnight and let her handle putting them to bed on her own. She was the nanny. That was her job. He had no business talking to her so much, or hanging around her room, or inviting her to dinners with people he was connected to on levels he hadn't let himself think much about. Yes, he'd take a huge step back. And as her boss, who happened to be an FBI agent, he could see if he could locate her cousin. He'd focus on that and nip any more personal discussion in the bud. A week from now they'd be leading very different lives; they would not be caring for Colt's nephews. They would not be staying at a romantic little inn in a quaint small town. They would not be a part of each other's lives.

He glanced over at Anna sitting beside him. She was looking out the passenger-side window, lost in thought.

Despite the long, dry pep talk he'd just given himself, he still wanted to know what she was thinking about.

"Good night," Colt said as they reached their rooms.

As she opened her door, she realized Colt wasn't planning on coming in to help get the babies settled. Not that he had to, but he'd done so last night at his condo.

She hurried in and set down Noah, then went back to the doorway where Colt stood, his expression unreadable, Nathaniel in his arms.

"'Night, buddy," he said to the baby. "You, too, Noah," he added as he handed the twin to Anna.

Something had changed. It was both subtle and overpowering, which made no sense. What had happened? Did the evening with his biological relatives make him uncomfortable? Maybe it was too much to process all at once and he needed some time to himself.

Or maybe he *had* heard her call him a kindred spirit and didn't like it. The phrase wasn't something she threw around, but since her little cousin Sadie was reading *Anne of Green Gables*, Anna had decided to also, and the main character, Anne, was fond of calling those who she felt a deep connection to kindred spirits. Sadie had declared Anna a kindred spirit, and Anna had worried about that. Anna Miller wasn't exactly a role model for a young Amish girl.

Or maybe she was. She truly wasn't sure about that yet. Anna had no business or right to lead Sadie to any conclusions that interfered with what her parents wanted for her. But Anna was who she was and couldn't try to be something else. That had never worked for her.

"If you need anything, I'll be in my room," Colt said, then nodded and headed into Room 2. He didn't look back as he closed the door behind him.

An ache settled in her stomach. She wanted him to help her put the boys to sleep, not because she couldn't do it on her own, but because she loved watching him interact with the twins, loved how his entire demeanor changed. He softened, he blew raspberries on bellies, he kissed wispy-haired heads. And after the boys would fall asleep, Anna loved talking to Colt, asking him about his job and his life in Houston. Tonight she'd hoped to talk more about Sarah and Jake and if he planned to welcome them into his life, but Colt had literally shut the door in her face. Politely enough, but still.

And she was hoping for a repeat of that kiss.

Definitely not happening tonight, she thought with a frown, looking at his closed door.

As Nathaniel gurgled in her arms, she held him

close, nuzzling his sweet head. "Let's get you changed, then your brother," she whispered.

Then maybe I'll have to change myself, she added silently. And stop this crazy crush on a man I'll never have.

Except once both boys were in their cribs and Anna began singing an English lullaby, she really wondered if she could have him…just once. Colt Asher was initiating her, so to speak, into his world, the English world, and could he not introduce her to the wonders and joys of sex? She would never meet a man like Colt Asher. She couldn't imagine ever feeling this lusty desire for another man. He was once-in-a-lifetime. Just like her *rumspringa*. This opportunity to know, to experience, to find out where she truly belonged.

She wouldn't proposition him, of course. But there was a week ahead of them. And *anything* could happen.

The thought thrilled her and terrified her.

Chapter Eight

A twin was stirring in his crib. Anna opened her eyes and stretched, then glanced at the alarm clock on the bedside table—5:03 a.m. Noah's little mouth was quirking, his eyes opening, and a moment later, Nathaniel was wide-awake.

"Who wants to be changed?" she asked, picking up Noah and laying him down on the padded dresser. A few minutes later, with Noah all set and in the playpen, she changed Nathaniel and set him next to his brother while she washed up and got dressed, poking her head out every minute to check on them. "Who wants breakfast? How about your favorite baby food and I'll have pancakes with strawberry slices?"

The very kind inn owner had let Anna know that she should make herself at home in the kitchen if she or the babies were hungry before breakfast hours or in the middle of the night. So after leaving a note for Colt on her door that she'd be in the kitchen, Anna scooped up a twin in each arm and headed down the hall, setting the boys in their baby seats at the kitchen table. Some Cheerios and tray toys would keep them busy, and Anna made breakfast, cutting up the pancakes and strawberries.

As she alternated between feeding the twins their fruit purees and eating her own breakfast, Anna was again hit with a pang so strong. She wanted to be a mother.

Maybe one night with Colt Asher shouldn't be on the horizon. Anna wanted a husband. A family. Wasn't this *rumspringa* about listening to her heart? If she wanted a family of her own she needed to work toward that goal. Not lust after an unattainable FBI agent who'd made it clear last night that there was nothing going on between them. He'd said their one kiss was a mistake. He'd meant it.

So wise up, Anna, she told herself.

After breakfast she took the boys back to her room to get the stroller and what she'd need for a walk through town. It was barely six thirty, but there were joggers and dog walkers out, and based on how they were dressed, it wasn't too chilly. Anna reached into her tote bag for the cell phone that Colt had bought her for their time in Blue Gulch. A quick touch to the weather app showed it was fifty-eight degrees this morning. Warm for the morning in this part of Texas in December. And just right for a brisk walk around town.

As she reached her room, she saw a note on the door.

Anna, will be back by 8:30 so you can make your appointment—Colt.

Was he avoiding her? Where could he have gone so early? Were coffee shops even open yet?

The realization that she hadn't been imagining his retreat made her heart sink. He *was* avoiding her. But he'd have to see her at eight thirty, when she handed over the babies. And maybe she'd get some answers then.

"All that looking around and people watching and seeing the Christmas tree on the town green tuckered out the twins," Anna said as Colt stepped inside her room at eight thirty. The hair salon was just a couple minutes' walk, so she'd have enough time to get there. "They're definitely ready for their morning nap."

"Perfect," he said. God, she looked so beautiful. The morning sun streamed through the filmy white curtains and lit one side of her face. She wore jeans and another of his sister's sweaters, a pale pink cardigan with a ruffled T-shirt under it. Her light blond hair was in a ponytail. She looked *so* young. She looked twenty-four. And thirty-two might not be anywhere near old, but sometimes he felt like he was a hundred.

"So you don't want to spend time with them?" she asked, her brown eyes on him. Her shoulders dropped. "Wait. I take that back. I'm picking a fight."

He smiled. "Why?"

She dropped down on the edge of the bed. "Because you disappeared on me last night. Suddenly things seem different between us, Colt."

He stared at her for a moment. "You really do put it out there, don't you?"

"I don't see the point of bottling stuff up or wondering or speculating. If you have a worry or concern or question, voice it."

Another thing he admired about her.

He might as well try it out for himself. "Last night— at Sarah's, dinner with everyone—was a lot for me to take in at once. I found myself actually opening up to Jake. Out of nowhere I started talking about my parents and their murder—payback from a criminal my father had arrested. I never talk about them or that night."

"Oh, Colt, I'm so sorry about what happened to your parents. You must feel comfortable around Jake if you told him."

"I don't think that's it. I don't really feel comfortable around anyone when I first meet them. Takes me a while to warm up."

"Nooo," she teased, a smile on her pretty face. "Though you did seem comfortable around me. Until the drive home."

More of that "putting it out there." He didn't really want to have this conversation. Mostly because he didn't really know how he felt about what she was asking. He could just say that. Put it out there, like she was.

"You should get going if you don't want to be late for your hair appointment" was what came out of his mouth, though. Colt was great at ending conversations.

"We're not done here, Colt Asher," she said.

I don't want to be done. But I don't want to start anything, either. I don't know what the hell I want where you're concerned.

But he didn't say that, either.

She seemed about to say something but then bit her lip and lifted her chin. Whatever it was, she was saving it up for next time.

"You're sure you're fine with watching them on your own?" she asked. "They usually nap for an hour and a half, but you never know. They both have a tooth coming in and the little pokes could wake them up."

"I've got this," he said. He had a general idea of what to do from watching his sister with the boys a few times and, of course, from seeing how Anna cared for them the past couple of days. He could probably handle one baby. But two? The twins would be lucky to have their diapers on only half-crooked, and Anna's room would probably be a mess by the time she returned. But maybe the twins wouldn't even wake up before she was back.

She headed over to the playpen, where the boys were playing with their little chew toys, their eyes definitely droopy. "'Bye, sweeties. See you soon." She pressed a kiss to her fingers and then each boy's head. She turned to Colt. "I'll see you in about an hour, I think."

"Don't rush back. Go shopping, explore the downtown. Have fun."

She tilted her head. Somehow he'd become pretty good at reading her. He could hear her thinking: *He doesn't want me to rush back so that we can't continue the conversation I started.*

She was only half-right. The other half wanted her to enjoy herself, have time to herself.

Because he cared about her.

The realization sent a chill up his spine. He did care about her. He wanted her to be happy. He wanted her to find what she was looking for while she was here. Which was herself.

A good reminder to stay far away from her. Emotionally and physically.

"Waaaah! Waah!"

Colt bolted up from where he sat at the desk in Anna's room. Nathaniel was sitting up, rubbing his eyes and crying. "What's wrong, little man?" Colt asked, rushing over and picking him up. Oh, wait—was he supposed to let Nathaniel try and soothe himself back to sleep? From all the eye-rubbing and sobbing going on, that didn't seem a real possibility anyway, and if Colt had let him cry, Nathaniel would wake up his slumbering brother.

Colt gave the direction of the baby's diaper a sniff. He smelled only powder, and gave a silent thanks. He offered Nathaniel his favorite chew toy to see if his incoming tooth was the problem, but the baby crumpled up his little face. "Okay, there, little guy, maybe your tummy's bothering you? Gas?" He laid Nathaniel on his back on the bed and tried Anna's bicycle-pump technique on the chubby legs, and got a "waaaah!" for the trouble. "So maybe you just want to be held and stretch out a little? Let's try that."

He picked up the baby and held him against his chest, one hand on the baby's bottom, the other gentle across Nathaniel's back, which he lightly rubbed. "The bitsy spider walked up the flowerpot," he sang, but the words didn't sound right. Nathaniel seemed to like his made-up version so he kept going.

Little eyes fluttered closed. Colt looked down at Nathaniel's beautiful face, his big cheek against his T-shirt.

So much trust. It was almost too much to bear. This tiny life was in Colt's hands.

Of course, now that he was itching to put Nathaniel back in his crib, he was afraid doing so would wake him up from Nap 2.0. "We'll just stay like this a little while," he whispered, gently rocking the baby in his arms.

His phone pinged with a text, and Colt walked back to the desk where he'd left it while getting information on Anna's cousin. He preferred having his tablet or laptop for any research he needed to do, but he'd vowed not to take along either while in Blue Gulch so that he couldn't easily get back in the Duvall crime syndicate's activities. He'd wanted to keep his head focused on the babies and getting to know Jake and Sarah. So texting his favors and checking databases on his phone would have to do to get intel on Mara Miller. Luckily, despite having one of the most common last names in the US, she had an uncommon enough first name. That, combined with details Anna had give him about her general age, made locating her a snap. She was right here in Texas. Three hours away, in Houston. All these years she'd been just fifteen minutes outside her village.

The text had nothing to do with Mara Miller, though. It was from his sister.

How's Uncle Colt? Boys okay? Pics?

Colt smiled and took a photo of each sleeping baby. All's well, he texted. Napping like champs. I hired an Amish nanny to help out. I now know how to handle baby gas and teething issues.

A smiley face emoji appeared. I owe you big, Cathy

texted back. Feels amazing to relax without a care, even though I miss my babies so much. See you soon and thank you!!!

He was surprised Cathy *had* been able to relax without a care with her boys as his charges. Yeah, he was an officer of the law. And an uncle with seven months of spotty experience. But her faith in him about babysitting for such a long stretch was strange. He wouldn't have trusted himself to do more than a C minus job. Which was why he'd hired Anna.

Though he had to admit he'd done okay just now. He'd handled Nathaniel's cries. He'd known what to do. That earned him an upgrade to maybe a B plus, maybe even an A minus. Anna would have gone straight for the A plus of letting Nathaniel stretch out vertically with a back rub before she had to try anything else. Next time, he assured himself.

He glanced down at the notes he'd taken on Mara Miller of Houston. She lived miles from where he did, in a not great section of the city. She worked as a waitress in a twenty-four-hour diner. Divorced, no kids. No arrests. A social-media photo showed a woman forcing a smile, as if trying to look happy. Colt was usually able to size up someone pretty easily, but he had no take on Mara Miller. For Anna's sake, he hoped she hadn't turned as bitter as the expression in her eyes suggested.

Nathaniel let out a little sigh and shifted his head. He seemed fast asleep, so Colt risked laying him down in his crib. The baby lifted up one chubby arm over his head in a little fist, his breathing indicating he wasn't waking up anytime soon. Success, yes!

Colt sat down in the rocker by the window, grabbing the squeaky stuffed bear before he could squish it.

His own eyes felt heavy. He'd gotten up early to avoid Anna and had gone for an early morning jog and then had explored the town on foot until the coffee shop opened. Since everyone was napping but him, he might as well close his eyes for a few minutes. Experience had proven one squawk from the babies would wake him up in two seconds.

His eyes closing, he thought of Anna. He wondered if she'd come back from the hair salon with a pixie cut like his sister had gotten after the two infants had yanked on her hair to the point she'd just cut it all off. Anna would look beautiful bald, he thought before drifting off.

"How much do you want cut off?" Sarah asked, running her fingers through Anna's waist-length hair as she stood behind her chair in the salon. "To start, maybe we should stick with a few inches past your shoulders. And then once you're used to that, you can go shorter. Or we can go for a big change at once."

Anna looked at herself in the big oval mirror on the wall. She still wasn't accustomed to looking at her reflection at all, but this focus on herself and how she looked didn't seem like vanity. She was here for a purpose, after all, to have her hair cut professionally for the first time ever. "Hmm. I do like it long. But I'm open to whatever you suggest. You're the professional."

"I know just what to do," Sarah said with a smile and picked up a pair of shiny silver scissors. But then she frowned, dropping her hand. "I just realized something, Anna. If you decide to return to your village after your *rumspringa*, perhaps you'll regret that your was hair cut? Maybe I should just give your ends a trim."

Anna looked at Sarah in the mirror. "You're very thoughtful, Sarah. But if I do go back, I'll have no regrets about my time in the English world. Nothing. Everything I experience here, everything I say yes to, will help me make my decision about going home or not. Having more 'English'-looking hair is part of that. Will I recognize myself with eight inches gone? Will the person in the mirror reflect how I feel on the inside? Or will she seem like a stranger? All questions that are getting answered one by one."

"Your English clothes suit you," Sarah said, lifting the scissors. "I would never have guessed you were Amish."

"I think no matter what happens when it's time for Colt to return his nephews, I'll always be Amish. Even if I stay in the English world and use electricity without a thought. There are things about the Amish lifestyle that are truly beautiful. Sometimes, simple is better. Sometimes, it's not. But the sense of community, of helping, of sharing, is wonderful."

Anna loved how easily she talked with Sarah. How easily she talked with anyone she'd met so far in Blue Gulch. Anna had always been reasonably outgoing and so usually "manned" the family and community stalls at the Amish market in Grass Creek, chatting away with the English about how the furniture was made and what type of paint was used and all the usual questions about the Amish and how they lived. Did they have outhouses? No, the Amish actually have toilets in their homes. Did they use utensils, or their hands to eat dinner? She would explain they have forks and knives just like the English. Did they get really bored not watching TV? Yes, sometimes. But it's not the Amish way to be bored. There's always someone to visit, work to do, pies to bake.

"Getting your Christmas shopping done, I see," Anna said, glancing at the big brown paper bag with wrapped gifts inside.

"Oh, I haven't started yet for the family. Those are for one of my Santa's Elves recipients."

"Santa's Elves?" Anna asked.

"The Hurley family started a new program in Blue Gulch—Santa's Elves. There are many families in town who can't afford to fix broken furnaces or sagging porches, let alone buy a turkey for Christmas dinner or gifts for children. So Essie Hurley—she owns Hurley's Homestyle Kitchen—put up flyers in her restaurant and in businesses around town to let folks know if they have any needs during the holiday season, from the serious to a wish for a particular present, to put their Christmas hopes in the Santa's Elves box on Hurley's porch. Those who are able to take on the wishes do so."

Anna loved the idea. "Can I be an elf? I'd love to help out while I'm here."

"Sure can. Just go on over to Hurley's after you leave here and pick a wish or two. If it's something you can't do yourself, like repaving a driveway, or is too expensive to hire out or buy, put it back and pick another that you can."

"It's a beautiful program," Anna said, glancing down at all the hair falling on the floor around the chair. "And very Amish. How are the wishes delivered?"

"You can leave physical gifts with a name tag with Essie Hurley at the restaurant. For services, you can arrange that and then let Essie know, and she'll inform the recipient that the wish has been granted. It is a really wonderful program."

Anna nodded. "I can't wait to pick a wish myself."

Sarah smiled and tilted Anna's head to the side while she snipped away. "Think those adorable twin babies are being good right now for their Uncle Colt?"

"I hope so. He's wonderful with them. He claims to not know much about babies or how to take care of them, but he's actually very natural at it."

"I noticed that last night. I'm so grateful to have this chance to get to know him."

For a moment Anna noticed that Sarah's pretty green eyes had misted with tears. How emotional this must be for her. Reunited—just this year—with both sons whom she'd given up for adoption thirty-two years ago.

"It was my one Christmas wish," Sarah said. "That I'd get to meet Colt. When Jake told me that he and his brother had tracked him down and that Colt had paid Jake a visit back in May, I was so hopeful that I'd get to meet him, too. And my wish was granted. It's one of the reasons why I want to help make others' Christmas wishes come true."

"I'm so glad," Anna said. "My Christmas wish is to find my cousin Mara while I'm in the English world. I don't know if it'll come true, but at least I have hope."

Sarah nodded. "Hope is everything." She put down the scissors and picked up a brush and blow-dryer.

"I've never had my hair blown dry before," Anna said, watching Sarah roll the brush down, the air shaft of the dryer following.

Sarah grinned. "You sure are going to experience a lot of firsts during this *rumspringa*."

Including my first broken heart, she thought, her

mind drifting to Colt. Granted, she knew what heart-ache felt like. She'd lost both parents. She'd hurt Caleb terribly when she'd turned him down and she'd felt her heart split in two. But she'd never felt romantic love for a man. Until the stirrings in her chest and belly and along her nerve endings indicated something was hap-pening inside her without her say-so at just the thought of Colt Asher.

Anna was so lost in thought about Colt that she hadn't even heard Sarah turn off the dryer or set it down.

"All done. And your hair looks amazing, if I do say so myself."

Anna looked in the mirror and gasped. "Wow. It does! I love it!" Her blond hair fell about three inches past her shoulders, and the front pieces were layered just a bit shorter than the rest so that it gave some lift and bounce. There was nothing fancy about the hair-style, but Anna still managed to look almost glamor-ous. It was perfect.

"You're a magician," Anna said. "Thank you so much, Sarah."

"It's my pleasure. And this is on me. Merry Christ-mas, Anna. Oh, and if you want some more pamper-ing, a mani-pedi or waxing, the salon does that, too."

A mani-pedi. Anna wasn't sure she would ever be ready to have someone polish her fingernails, let alone her toenails, but the idea of sparkly red fingernails made her happy. Some things were very temporary—like her job. Like nail polish. And some things weren't. Like tattoos and the way she felt about Colt Asher.

As Anna headed back up Blue Gulch Street, she passed the inn and darted up the steps to Hurley's

Homestyle Kitchen. The restaurant was closed, but Anna could see the kitchen crew at work through the big windows of the kitchen. A bright red metal box was on the porch railing. Santa's Elves Wishes was written across the front in black marker. Anna opened up the box and pulled out a folded piece of paper.

If someone could help patch my roof, I'd appreciate it. When it rains, I put a bucket on the floor but I slipped yesterday and hurt myself so bad I couldn't even get to work today.
Amanda Lottertin, 23 Hunter Way.

Anna would certainly get that taken care of. Help is on the way, Amanda! She reached in the box and picked out another folded wish.

Dear Santa, my name is Sophie. I'm eight. I saw a doll in the toy store and it had red hair like me. I'm the only one with red hair in my class. I want that doll more than anything else in the whole world.
Love, Sophie.
I live on Mannox Street. Do you know where that is, Santa?

Anna's heart squeezed at the thought of the girl's red hair. Like her cousin Sadie's. She missed Sadie so fiercely.

She would take both wishes and make them come true. She had money saved and could afford to have the roof patched. And she would certainly buy that red-haired doll in the toy store. If she wasn't mistaken, the toy store was across the street, near the coffee shop.

She glanced at her watch. She'd been gone an hour and a half so far. Should she take Colt at his word not to rush back? She'd just need another fifteen minutes to buy the doll and have it wrapped.

As she approached the toy store, she saw the doll in the window. She'd love to buy one for her cousin, too, but the Amish didn't allow dolls with faces. Amish dolls were homemade, adorable rag dolls who wore Amish-style clothes. The lack of faces was to show youngsters that all were the same in the eyes of God. Anna had never been too sure of that notion, though. All were alike inside, but every boy and girl, every man and woman, looked different on the outside.

Anna bought the doll and had it wrapped and wrote a card with Sophie's name and address on it. She'd deliver it to Hurley's when they were open. And she'd ask around about who to hire to fix Amanda Lottertin's roof and get that going today.

Back at the inn, Anna quietly opened her door just in case the twins were sleeping. She smiled as she stepped inside. The boys *were* sleeping. *All* of them. Colt was sprawled out on the overstuffed chair by the window, a stuffed bear on his lap.

She tiptoed in, putting the gift on the desk, then sat down on the chair. There was a piece of paper on the desk—with her cousin's name.

Mara Miller. 24 Huxton Road #4. Houston. 555-2365.

Anna gasped and covered her hand with her mouth. Had Colt found Mara? The thought of her cousin, on her own out here all these years, had haunted her ever since her aunt had told her about Mara. Of course, Mara was likely not alone; she'd probably married, had a family, had good friends and a full life. But she'd said goodbye to one life that didn't fit for another that she hoped would. Like Anna was doing right now. Had the English world suited her cousin? Anna hoped so. Because Mara had never come home.

Now, here was her name and an address and a telephone number.

You're making my Christmas wish come true, she thought, staring at the beautiful man asleep on the chair.

It wasn't very Amish of her that another Christmas wish was poking at her heart. To have this man, too.

Chapter Nine

Colt woke up to find Anna sitting at the desk chair, staring out the window. She seemed lost in thought. The sun streaming in lit up her gorgeous blond hair, which now fell a few inches past her shoulders and looked like spun silk. He had the urge to go over and run his fingers through it, carry her to the bed and slowly undress her...

As if she could feel him staring at her she turned and smiled. "Morning, sleepyhead. Glad you got a little nap in."

"Your hair is gorgeous," he said without thinking.

"Sarah is a magician." She touched the ends and grinned, and he knew she was very happy with her new look.

"Got some Christmas shopping done?" he asked, gesturing at the wrapped gift on the desk beside her.

Perhaps that meant she planned to return to her village, after all. Though, of course she would return for Christmas. He knew that the Amish had shunning practices, but he wasn't sure for what. If someone didn't return from *rumspringa* and left the faith and community, were they not allowed back? Could their family speak to them again? He had no idea what she was facing if she chose to live in the English world.

"I did, yes. Sarah told me about a new program called Santa's Elves." She explained about the box set up at Hurley's and choosing two wishes. "I wonder who I could speak to about a referral for the roof work," she said. "In my village, I'd mention it to my uncle, and word would spread quickly that someone's roof needed patching. It would be done within a day."

"Let me text Jake. He's lived here for months now. He'll know who to hire." He liked having a good reason to contact his twin. Sending a "Hey, how's it going?" or "Meet for coffee tomorrow?" seemed weird. He picked up his phone and sent off a text about Anna's request, glad to know he'd encouraged more contact, even if it was just about a roof referral. It was a start.

Anna smiled. "The wrapped gift is a doll for a little girl who fell in love with a red-haired doll in the window of the toy store. Like your boss's niece fell in love with Sparkles in the pet-shop window."

"I forgot all about Sparkles," he said. "Lots else on my mind." Though how could he forget the black-and-white guinea pig who'd brought him and Anna together? Without Anna, he'd be on his own with the boys, probably too flustered by his duties as an uncle to deal well with getting to know his twin and birth mother. Not that he was dealing all that well, regardless. "I'd like to grant a few wishes, too."

"We can stop by Hurley's," she said. "Or you can," she added quickly, giving him the out of not going together.

"Well, there is somewhere I'd like to take you," he said. "So why don't we stop by Hurley's before we head out?"

"Where?" she asked.

"Did you see the paper on the desk?" he asked, gesturing at it.

She nodded. "I was about to ask. You found my cousin?"

"She wasn't hard to find. Of course, without a social security number I can't be one-hundred-percent sure she's the right Mara Miller, but she's the right age. And I can see you in the photo I saw on a social-media account."

"Will you show me?"

He pulled up the Facebook account. Mara Miller wasn't much of a poster. There were some shots of sunsets. A squirrel eating an acorn in a tree. A bible quote. And her profile photo.

Anna took the phone and stared at the picture. "She looks like a Miller, for sure. And though she's smiling, the smile doesn't reach her eyes, does it?"

"No," he agreed. "According to what I could find out, she lives in Houston—in a run-down area. She works as a waitress in a twenty-four-hour diner. She's divorced, no children."

"No children?" Anna repeated, frowning. "I mean, not every woman wants children. Or can have children. I guess I'm just surprised. I don't know why, though.

I have to shift my way of thinking. Not everyone or everything has to be traditional."

"I thought we'd drive out to her diner during her shift and get a sense of her before you decide if you want to introduce yourself. She's related, Anna, but you've never met her. You don't know anything about her except that she left your village before you were born."

"What is there to know? She's my cousin. She's *Onkel* Eli's late brother's daughter."

"I'm an FBI agent. My instinct is to investigate first. Always."

"Okay," she said. "But I'd be fine with just calling her. Although I wonder if she'd even want to talk to me. Maybe she wants no reminders of her childhood, her past."

"And maybe she'll be overjoyed to hear your name," he said, surprising even himself.

The smile that lit her face warmed his wary heart.

Colt and Anna wheeled the twins' stroller over to Hurley's, and Anna waited on the sidewalk while Colt went up to the porch to deliver the doll to Essie and then pull some wishes from the Santa's Elves box for himself to fulfill. He took out a raggedly ripped-out sheet of notebook paper, the wish written in black script that wasn't too easy to read.

My name is Thomas McDougal. I want to pro-pose to my girlfriend but I'm short seventy-seven dollars for the ring I have on layaway. I know this is asking a lot, but if you can spare seventy-seven dollars, you can bring it to Blue Gulch Jewelers and add it to my account. My fiancée is a single

mother of two little boys and doesn't have any
jewelry at all so I really want to get her something special. I work full-time as a mechanic at
Johnny's Auto but between rent and bills, I can't
come up with the rest on the ring by Christmas.
Thank you.

Was someone cutting onions nearby? Jesus. Straight
to the heart. Colt tucked the note in his pocket. He'd
definitely take care of the seventy-seven bucks.

He pulled out one more wish from the box.

To Santa. Like you exist. Ha! I'm eleven, not five.
I know Santa isn't real. But if you're real you can
bring my sister another ballerina snow globe because I broke hers by accident even though she
said I did it on purpose. She cried for two days.
I'll give up my present so she can have a new
snow globe—From: Brady Canby

Been there myself, Brady, he thought, tucking that
note in his pocket, too. Oh, hell, maybe he'd pull one
more.

But since Anna was waiting and they had a long trip
ahead—one that was emotionally fraught—he wanted
to get on the road. So he pulled three more wishes and
stuffed them in his pocket. He'd read them later.

"Hey, Colt!"

Colt turned around to find his twin and his wife
waving as they approached from the opposite direction. Jake had baby Violet in a sling across his chest.

"I'm glad we ran into you," Jake said. "I wanted to
invite you two over for lunch today, if you're free. My

ranch hands are headed to a seminar on spring calv-
ing, so it's just me and Emma."

"I've love to, but I found Anna's cousin and we're
going to drive to Houston today to see her."

"That's great that you found her," Jake said. "Anna
must be relieved."

"She is. Of course, she has no idea what to expect
when we do meet her. So she's excited and nervous."

"We'd be happy to babysit the twins if it would be
easier to travel without the babies," Emma said.

Huh. It would be a lot easier. He could focus his
attention completely on Anna, and Anna could focus
her attention on meeting Mara and what she was feeling, rather than being distracted by the twins. "You're
sure? Double the trouble. Though they are easy babies."

"We'd love to. Plus, we'll get to see what our daughter will be doing in about six months."

Colt smiled. "Okay, but it's six hours' travel and a
few hours there. That's all day. You're *sure* you want
two more babies at the ranch?"

"We're absolutely sure," Jake said. "We'll take good
care of them. Go on your trip." He leaned down and
waved at Anna in Jake's car.

She opened her door and stepped out. "Hi, nice to
see you both again."

"These crazy kids are going to take the twins for
the day so that we can focus on our trip," Colt said to
Anna. He took the car seats from the SUV and installed
them in Jake's—the three car seats fit perfectly. With
the twins' bag already packed with everything they'd
need for the day, Anna handed that over, too.

"Wow, thank you," Anna said.

"I really appreciate this," Colt added. "It'll make today a lot easier on us."

Jake smiled. "Of course. That's what—" Colt thought Jake was about to say *that's what family is for*, but if he was, he stopped himself.

Colt shook Jake's hand. "I'll text you when we're on our way back."

And just like that, he and Anna were baby-free for the day.

As he got back inside his car, he turned to Anna. "Strangest darn thing."

"What?"

"I trust Jake with my baby nephews. I barely know him, but I trust him one hundred percent."

It wasn't like Colt to trust. But he'd had the same feeling about Anna, too. Trust. A sense deep inside that he couldn't explain. Now he had the same feeling about Jake Morrow.

What the heck was happening to him? In any case, it felt strangely good.

Anna smiled and squeezed his hand. "What wish did you get from the Santa's Elves box?"

He told her about the engagement ring. About grumbly Brady Canby, who didn't believe in Santa anymore. About the three other notes he took but didn't read.

"You're going to grant five wishes?" she asked. "That's generous."

"If I can," he said, starting the ignition and then pulling away. "If any of the three I picked unread are outrageous and asking for a Lamborghini, that's something else."

She smiled, but he could see that she was distracted and nervous.

"You okay?" he asked.

She shrugged. "All these years I've been fighting against 'knowing what to expect.' It's one of the reasons why I want to live in the English world. Adventure. Experiences. But suddenly I don't know what I'll be facing when we find Mara. I don't even know if she'll want to meet me."

"You're her cousin," she said. "You're family. There's a connection there. It's highly likely she will want to meet you. Even I wanted to meet my birth relatives."

She smiled. "That's true. I hope you're right. I can't imagine leaving home at seventeen—and such a sheltered home—and not seeing your family for almost twenty-five years. I was hoping she'd have her own huge family to make up for it, but you said she was divorced and childless."

"Could she have come back?" he asked. "You can, why can't she?"

"I haven't been baptized into the Amish faith. Therefore, I can't really break any rules. I can't be excommunicated if I haven't been baptized. Though by twenty-five, if you haven't been baptized, you'll be pressured to. That has already started with me. But Mara was baptized when she was sixteen. My aunt told me that she had a very short *rumspringa*, she much preferred the Amish life, and officially joined the church. But then she left the following year. Because she left, she was excommunicated. If she did come back, my family would be expected to shun her."

Colt frowned. "So her relatives would act like she doesn't exist?"

"Not as bad as that, but bad. She wouldn't be able to

share the same dining table with the Millers. That kind of thing. Unless, of course, she admitted her wrong-doing at church and publicly asked for forgiveness, the shunning period would be brief."

Shunning went on in his world, too, unfortunately. Maybe not the church-ordained kind, but there had been plenty of the ol' cold shoulder in his house as he grew up.

"Was it about a guy?" he asked. "The reason Mara left?"

"I asked my aunt and she said Mara hadn't been dating anyone. Mara always kept to herself, so perhaps she was dating an Englisher and no one knew it. That was one of the rumors." She shrugged. "Everyone figured she'd gotten pregnant. But I guess not."

"Well, we will soon meet Mara and all your questions will be answered." He hoped, anyway.

She smiled, but turned toward the window, so he gave her some privacy with her thoughts. He wanted to reach out, caress her face, her shoulders, just to let her know he cared, that he was here for her, but perhaps it was better that he kept his hands to himself.

As signs for Houston appeared on the highway, Anna felt butterflies fluttering in her stomach. Suddenly she realized how close they were to Grass Creek. Maybe she could catch a sighting of her family at the Amish market. She glanced at her watch. The timing was right. She'd hang back, tuck up her hair in the cute knit hat she'd bought in Blue Gulch this morning, put on the sunglasses she'd gotten from the same store and just soak in the sight of Kate and Sadie. Even Eli would be a welcome familiar sight, she thought with a smile. Seeing her family, the familiar, would help ease her anxiety about meeting Mara. She'd feel a bit more grounded, more...herself.

"Colt, would you mind stopping near the Amish market in Grass Creek? I don't want to go in and say hello; I just want to hang back and see my family from afar. With my haircut, these clothes and sunglasses, I can stand back and observe. Just get a glimpse of them. I sure would love to lay eyes on Sadie, even for a few minutes."

Colt nodded and turned off for the Grass Creek exit. En route to the market, they passed a few buggies. The Amish market was at the end of the bustling downtown, a small park near the entrance. Colt parked and Anna took a deep breath.

Anna tucked her hair up inside the pretty red hat, put on her big black sunglasses and stepped out. She took a look around—several buggies were parked near the entrance to the market, but she didn't see the Millers'. Another two buggies turned the corner and one parked.

"Oh, my goodness, there they are!" Anna gestured with her chin at her uncle Eli getting down from the buggy and going around to the back of the wagon. A pair of red pigtails poked out the back and skinny arms lifted up a pale yellow baby cradle and handed it to Eli. Kate was just visible in the buggy, staying in it while Eli and Sadie each carried two cradles up the path to the market.

Anna watched Sadie stare at an English girl doing cartwheels on the grassy area alongside the path to the entrance. According to the Amish, if you had time for cartwheels, you certainly had time to help with cooking or laundry or cleaning or minding a toddler for a sick *mamm*. When Sadie and her father returned for another batch of small pieces, Sadie said something to her dad and Eli frowned, but then he nodded and stopped walking. Sadie attempted to do a cartwheel. Anna heard the English girl call out that Sadie had to push off with her arms and keep her legs straight. Eli nodded at Sadie, who gave it another try and did much better. Sadie's grin lit up her whole face, and Anna missed her little cousin so much. And Eli had surprised her. Anna wondered if her leaving had actually made him soften just a bit where Sadie was concerned, let her have a bit of her curiosity sated instead of scorned. It wasn't often that Anna felt a surge of affection for her stern uncle, but she did now.

Anna hurried back to the car. "I had good luck here. So I'm going with the notion that I'll have good luck in Houston when I see Mara."

He smiled and started the car and they took off, Anna looking back for a last glimpse of the Millers, but she didn't see them.

"Did seeing your family make you long to go home?" he asked as he took a Houston exit off the freeway.

"I don't know. I sure do miss them. But there's a lot I haven't explored out here in your world. A lot I haven't experienced," she added, looking at him as she imagined a second kiss, even more passionate than the first.

She felt herself blush. Did he know what she was thinking? He probably did. He was a face reader. And good at his job, no doubt.

"I mean, how could I even think of returning home when I haven't experienced Mexican food. Indian food.

Or Thai." That was a quick save, she thought, giving herself a pat on the back.

"I love Thai. Let's have that for lunch."

She grinned. And was grateful that if he had known the lascivious turn her thoughts had taken, he'd let her off the hook. Colt was good that way. Anna was discovering that *she* was the pusher of conversations *he* didn't want to have.

As Colt drove, Anna became aware that the area they were in wasn't as nice. There were boarded-up buildings. Graffiti. Garbage on the street.

"There's the diner Mara works in," he said, pointing up ahead. Colt parked and they walked across the street to the diner. The small brick building looked inviting enough. The door was painted bright red. A big sign in the window read:

This is a restaurant where you pay what you can. No one will be turned away for not having enough money for a meal.

Anna stared at the sign, then looked at Colt. "It's a mission," she said with a smile. She pulled open the door and they headed in. The diner was tiny with a ten-seat counter and ten tables. There were two waitresses and two cooks visible through the open area to the kitchen behind the counter. Five of the tables were taken, and four seats at the counter.

"Can I help you folks?" asked a waitress.

"Two for lunch," Colt said. "If Mara's working today, we'd like a table in her section."

The woman led them over to a table by the window and handed them each a menu. There were no prices.

The cover of the menu said, "Pay what you feel your meal is worth. If you can't pay, that's okay, too. Funded by the Houston Together Initiative."

Another waitress came over. She had blond hair just past her chin and blue eyes. She was tall and slender and wore a bright yellow apron with the words Houston Together Diner on it. Her name tag read Mara. "What can I do for you folks today?" she asked.

Anna sucked in a breath. This was her cousin! She most definitely looked like a Miller. "I'd love to hear a bit about how the diner works."

"Ditto," Colt said.

"You'll see our menu is limited. We generally always have burgers and grilled cheese and egg dishes. With our daily donations, we create a specials board, and today we have three soups. Minestrone, chicken noodle and my personal favorite, Hungarian mushroom."

"Say no more," Colt said. "I'll have the mushroom soup and a burger with the works."

"Me, too," Anna said. She handed the menus back to Mara.

Mara smiled, jotted their orders down on her little notepad and headed behind the counter, where she spoke in diner shorthand to the cooks.

She returned with two bowls of steaming soup. "Here you go. Enjoy."

Anna smiled at her. "Thank you. May I ask—this is a mission, right?"

Mara nodded. "There are many homeless people in this neighborhood who won't go to soup kitchens or shelters. We're essentially a soup kitchen masquerading as a diner. We have a band of volunteers to keep the place going. We're doing pretty well. We've been written up in a few local papers about how good our soups and burgers are, so we attract paying customers in addition to those who can't. We open at four o'clock on Christmas Eve and we're open all day on Christmas. That way, everyone has somewhere to go."

"That's wonderful," Anna said. As Mara turned to go, Anna said, "Mara?"

The waitress turned.

"My name is Anna Miller. I'm Rebecca and Robert Miller's daughter. My *aenti* and *onkel* are Kate and Eli."

Mara gasped. "Did you come here specifically to find me?"

"Well, I'm taking a very late *rumspringa*," Anna said. "And I'd always wondered what became of you. You left right before I was born. So while I was out and about in the English world, I thought I'd look you up. You were easier to find than I expected. Though it helps to have an FBI agent as a boss."

Mara looked at Colt, her eyes wide.

Anna explained how she and Colt met, leaving out the part about Sadie taking the guinea pig. "And here I am."

"Will you go back after your week is up?" Mara asked.

"I don't know. From Colt's car I saw Kate and Eli and their daughter at the Amish market before we came here. I miss them so much. Can I ask why you left?"

Mara bit her lip. "Give me a few minutes to take care of some customers and I'll be back."

Anna watched her cousin pour coffee for two tables

and check on the others. Then Mara returned with their burgers and sat down.

"When I was seventeen, I fell madly in love with an Englisher while working at my family stall at the market. I would sneak out to meet him. The bishop's daughter caught us making out behind the market. I wasn't her favorite person. She told me that she'd report me and I'd be shunned and no one in my family could talk to me. And that I'd bring shame on them so that I should just leave. I'd been baptized just a few months prior, but I was so in love with the English guy that I decided to leave. My parents were gone and I was living with Eli's father, who was very strict. So I decided to leave to save everyone trouble."

"Do you ever want to go back?" Anna asked.

"To be honest, I feel that I can do good work here," she said. "I run this diner and also a free day-care program staffed by volunteers. And every summer I do missionary work across Texas. I love my life. It's not easy, but I love it. I feel like I'm doing what I was born to do."

Doing what I was born to do... Anna wondered if she'd ever feel that way. "I'm so glad, Mara. You found your calling."

Mara nodded. "I am very glad to meet you, though, Anna. It always feels good to connect with a piece of home. Even after all these years."

"Can we keep in touch?" Anna asked. "I'd love to spend more time together."

"Of course," Mara said. "But if you go home and commit to the faith, your life will be there. It won't extend past the village."

"Do you ever miss that? How simple and quiet life was?"

Mara nodded. "Definitely. But I feel like myself in the English world."

"Did you marry that English boy?" Anna asked, hoping that wasn't too personal.

"I did. It didn't work out. But I have a terrific boyfriend now. He's one of the volunteer cooks here. I never expected a highfalutin tax attorney to want to help cook, let alone take care of our books, but there he is, making the best hash browns I've ever had."

Anna smiled. "I'm so glad. Things sure worked out for you, Mara."

A small group of people came in. "No complaints. I'd better get back to work." She wrote down her information on a card and handed it to Anna. "Call me anytime."

Anna took the card and carefully put it in her wallet. She watched Mara hand the newcomers menus. Her cousin smiled but there was fatigue in her expression, which was what Anna and Colt had observed in Mara's social-media photo. The woman was quite understandably tired from all she did to help her community.

Colt took a bite of the burger. "She wasn't kidding about the burger. Delicious. Soup, too."

Anna glanced down. She'd been so busy talking that she hadn't eaten much. She ate a bit more of her burger and some soup, but her appetite had left her.

"A lot to take in," he said.

"She really made her own life," Anna said. "Her way. I'm very impressed."

Colt nodded. "Me, too. Just yesterday I was thinking that I hate not knowing what to expect, but sometimes, people really do surprise you in a good way. I thought we'd be meeting someone who'd gotten knocked around by life. But here we have someone dedicating her life to helping others." When Mara returned and started clearing their plates, and set down their bill, Colt put a hundred-dollar bill on the check.

Mara came over and gasped. "Please tell me you want change."

Colt shook his head. "It's my pleasure. Merry Christmas."

They shook hands, and then Anna wrapped her cousin in a hug. "I'm so glad I got to meet you, Mara. You're an inspiration."

The woman smiled. "You are, too."

Hardly, Anna thought as she and Colt headed out. What was Anna doing with her life? How was she helping anyone?

One step at a time, she reminded herself. *You did leave your village for this...trial experience. You don't even know if you're staying or going back home.*

"I kept thinking there was an 'either-or,'" Anna said as they got into Colt's SUV. "Either I stay in the English world, or I go home and commit to being Amish. But it's not about the English or Amish world. It's about what I want to do with my life."

Colt turned on the ignition and then pulled into traffic. "Like you said, you have a lot to explore, a lot of experiences awaiting you, Anna Miller. But your cousin is right—you *are* an inspiration. Leaving everything you know takes guts."

"I don't feel brave. I feel a little off-kilter most of the time."

"I'd think that goes with the territory. I mean, the

things I take for granted, like flipping a light switch, like relying on a cell phone, like wearing what I please, are new to you. But it's more than that. Anyone can learn new technologies and get used to anything. Whether you'll stay is about here," he said, pressing a hand to his heart. "That's how you'll really know where you'll belong."

"You keep surprising me," she said. "I don't expect you to be talking about what the heart knows and all that."

He glanced at her with a raised eyebrow. "I do *have* a heart."

She smiled and wanted to throw her arms around him. "I know." *But it's bigger than you realize and has more room than you think. So let me in!*

"Can I ask you something, Colt?"

"Of course."

Just say it, she told herself. *You don't get the answer if you don't ask the question.* "If I do decide to stay in your world...you won't necessarily be around. Right?"

As he stopped for a red light, he looked at her for a long moment, then turned his attention back to the road. "I'll be on a case."

"So, that's what you decided you want to do with your life—work?"

"Work getting criminals off the street and behind bars, yes."

"But that doesn't have to be your *whole* life," she said.

"It doesn't have to be. I want it to be."

She nodded, slowly, aware she was trying to fight the truth. *When someone tells you who and what they are, believe them.* Her mother used to say that. Colt was telling her he wasn't the marrying kind, the family kind, the settling-down kind. He lived for his job. Or that she just wasn't the one. So she should believe him and forget about a future with Colt Asher.

Except she was falling further in love with him every day.

Anna Miller also had a saying. It went like this: fight for what you want.

There were two sides to Colt Asher. The first: the lone-wolf FBI agent who needed no one. The second: the loving man who'd saved his sister's much-needed vacation, gave up his own, changed an Amish woman's life—and helped a little Amish girl by not ratting her out—with a job offer, was a great uncle and babysitter, a superb tipper and all-around generous human being.

The latter was a longer list. Anna wasn't giving up on him.

Chapter Ten

As they approached the exit for Blue Gulch, Colt pulled over to text Jake and let him know that they'd be at the ranch in about twenty minutes to pick up the twins.

The little guys are fast asleep, Jake texted back. Why not pick them up in the morning? Enjoy the evening.

Huh. "Looks like we have the night off from baby duty," he said to Anna.

"Aww, I miss the twins. And it feels strange to be apart from them for so long after taking care of them round-the-clock for a few days."

"I know what you mean. I feel a little itchy about it, to be honest. Like something is missing."

Anna smiled. "You love them."

"Duh," he said. "I'm their uncle."

"Yes, but you *looove* them. They're inside your heart. Under your skin."

He wasn't quite sure what she was getting at and wasn't sure he wanted to know. "It doesn't make sense to wake them up just to bring them home and have them be all grouchy. We should let them sleep."

"Agreed," she said. "You know what I would love to do on our night off? Have that pad Thai you mentioned earlier. See a movie in a theater—that would be a first for me. I've never dressed up for a night out. I've never worn earrings or lipstick."

This would be...like a date. He swallowed.

"But it wouldn't be a date," he said quickly. "Just a night out."

He caught her frown before she could hide it. Unfortunately, he was well trained to catch every minute facial movement. Now he felt like a jerk.

"Well, it could be *like* a date," she said. "I've never been on a date in the English world. You could show me what I'd be in for."

"In for?" he asked. Now he was the one frowning.

"Well, if I stay in your world, I'll need to know what I'm getting into. What English men are like, what is done on dates, how things go."

He hadn't really considered the idea of Anna dating. But of course she would. Why did it bug him?

Hmm. Maybe he should take her out on a date. It would give him a chance to sort out his feelings for her, which were all over the place. He'd be sitting across from her in the Thai place instead of in their rooms with babies and their stuff all around them. He'd have more of a chance to see her as a woman and not his nanny. Given how young she was—eight years his junior—and how sheltered, he was sure he'd see that she would be better suited to a younger, more sheltered kind of guy, someone more her...type. Surely he wasn't it.

"Date night, it is," he said. "It's almost five thirty now. Why don't I pick you up at seven?"

She laughed. "By walking across the hall and knocking on my door?" she asked.

"Yes."

She laughed again and for a moment he was mesmerized by her big smile and the happiness in her brown eyes.

"Well, then," he said as he parked in the lot for their inn. "I will see you at seven."

"See you at seven," she repeated. But instead of going inside the inn, she turned left and walked down Blue Gulch Street. He wondered where she was going.

He saw her pause in front of a shop window and look at something, then go inside. As he turned to enter the inn, his gaze stopped on Blue Gulch Jewelers. He could dash inside and pay off Thomas McDougal's ring. He liked the idea of the man knowing, as soon as possible, that it was taken care of so he could plan his big proposal.

God, maybe Colt was getting soft.

He crossed the street and entered the shop, the bell jangling overhead. He explained to the saleswoman what he wanted to do.

"Oh, that's just wonderful!" she said, touching her heart as he handed over the cash. "Would you like to leave a note for him?" She brought over a pad of stationery with the jewelry shop's logo across the top.

For Thomas McDougal,
Merry Christmas!
—Santa's elf

The saleswoman smiled. "Short and sweet. Can I
help you with anything else?"

Colt was about to say no and leave, but he noticed
a pair of earrings on display and thought about what
Anna had said about having never worn earrings before.

"I'd like to buy a pair of earrings, but I don't think
the recipient has pierced ears."

"Ah, then you want clip-ons. We don't have many
but we do have a few beauties." She opened the display
case and pulled out a tray.

Right away, Colt knew the ones Anna would love.
He didn't know how he knew, considering he had no
clue what her style was. She was wearing his sister's
clothes, after all. But the gold earrings, with their delicate filigree leaf pattern, slightly dangling, were *her*.
"I'll take those."

With the gift in a white box with velvet backing,
Colt left and headed back to the inn. He pressed his ear
to Anna's door but didn't hear any movement.

Were the earrings too much? Too intimate? He didn't
think so. But what if she took them the wrong way and
thought the gift meant more than that he wanted her to
have a special night?

Did they mean more? Hell, he wasn't even sure himself. He could have bought her flowers, yellow roses,
something friendly. But he went for jewelry.

Because she'd said something about earrings! he
yelled silently to himself. *Not intimate. Just a friendly
gesture.*

* * *

Anna glanced at the price tag of the shoes she'd fallen in love with in the window of the boutique. They were half price as part of a big Christmas sale. Leather peep-toe, three inches and incredibly sexy. They would go so nicely with the black wrap dress she'd brought from Colt's sister's closet. For her one big night out, she would treat herself.

She wondered whether she'd have a chance to wear them again. Or if she'd return to her village, the shoes hidden in the back of her closet as a memory. She still couldn't say either way. Her heart was in the English world. But it was also back home. Maybe because that was where her only family was. Her dear young cousin, Sadie.

But she could visit with no repercussions on her family. She hadn't committed to the faith, so leaving it was not an issue. The bishop and the other families wouldn't be happy with the news, but sometimes, that was how it went and it was accepted.

Could she live out here in this world where these shoes were probably in every woman's closet? The thought was actually very exciting. Yes, she could. And she wanted to. Wearing sexy shoes and lipstick didn't mean she was vain. Looking in a mirror didn't mean she was vain, either. She thought of Mara, doing so many wonderful things for her community. There was a balance, and Anna would like to find it for herself.

She bought the shoes.

And in the intimates section, where there was a display of bras and panties, she bought a matching lacy black set. Fine, she was a giant step ahead of herself. But who knew? Maybe they'd be flung off her body tonight in a fit of passion. Maybe Colt Asher would never see the sexy lacy bra and underwear at all. Either way, maybe they'd join the shoes in the back of her closet, never to be seen again except in her memories. In any case, she was buying them.

In the drugstore a few doors down she found the cosmetics aisle. Lipstick, definitely. A sheer red, nothing crazy. A brown mascara and an eyeliner pencil for a bit of that "smoky eye" she read about in magazines while in Grass Creek. She had the shoes. The makeup. The undergarments. She wouldn't mind buying a bracelet or earrings to complete her outfit, but it was almost six fifteen and she'd barely have time to get ready. She did take one of the perfume samples at the counter. It was aptly called Seduction.

A thrill racing up and down her nape, she hurried back to the inn, loving how it felt to be carrying bags, even if one was just from the drugstore. As she approached her room, she eyed Colt's door, goose bumps popping up on her arms and nape at the thought of him taking her out on the town.

She knew in the car, as they'd been stopped on the side of the road while he texted Jake, that she had her *in* with him. When she'd said she missed the twins and that it felt strange to be apart from them, he hadn't looked at her as though she had two heads. He hadn't raised an eyebrow and said, "Are you kidding? A night of freedom awaits!" No. He'd said, "I feel a little itchy about it, to be honest. Like something is missing."

Whether he wanted to acknowledge it or not, she knew that Noah and Nathaniel had shown Colt a side of himself he didn't know well—a side he might not have believed was there in him at all.

The man was not a lost cause. He felt deeply. He cared. He loved those little nephews of his. And he missed them. He did, indeed, have a heart—a big one—and while she was here with him, she'd make it her mission to show Colt he could have so much more than a job and an empty condo to come home to.

And tonight could be her only opportunity to have Colt Asher to herself and to experience a "date night." Although, she was pretty sure that phrase was used for married people. She liked it, though.

She was having "date night," and she was going to make the most of it.

At seven on the dot, Colt knocked on Anna's door. She opened the door, and his eyes almost popped out of his head.

She was smoking hot.

Anna. The woman he'd met in baggy overalls and a baseball cap. The woman he'd hired while wearing a loose blue dress up to her neck and down to her ankles, a white bonnet on her hair. The woman who'd been in jeans and a sweater and sneakers and not a stitch of makeup.

He was speechless. She wore a slinky black dress and incredibly sexy high-heeled shoes. There was a hint of cleavage—and the hint was driving him wild. As was the subtle scent of perfume.

"You look absolutely beautiful, Anna."

She smiled and he could barely take his eyes off her glossy red mouth.

Earth to Colt. Snap out of it! "Before we head out… I got you a little something," he said, handing her the white box.

"Colt! You didn't have to do that." She opened the box and bit her lip. "Earrings. They are so lovely."

"You just clip them right on," he said a bit sheepishly, unsure if she had any idea how to do that.

"Come on in," she said. "I need a mirror for this first attempt at wearing earrings."

He followed her in, watching her smile in the reflection of the mirror over the bureau. She put down the box and took out an earring and clipped it on, moving her hair to take a look in the mirror. "I love them! The leaf is so pretty." She attached the other one and turned left and right, admiring them in the mirror. "Thank you so much, Colt. My outfit feels complete now."

The dangling gold earrings suited her. One side of her hair was pushed behind her ear, and he was overcome with the urge to kiss her neck.

"You're very welcome. Just a little something to celebrate your first big night out in the English world. And to say thank you for being such a great nanny. I couldn't have lasted these few days without you, Anna. And there are a few more to go."

She was quiet for a moment, then said, "Good, because I adore those little nephews of yours." She cleared her throat and suddenly seemed a little uncomfortable. "Shall we go?"

He nodded, wondering what he'd said wrong. "We can walk to the Thai restaurant. It's at the end of Blue Gulch Street. I know it's not the same as being escorted around in a Jag, but it's a nice night for a walk."

She looped her arm through his, the simple touch sending shock waves through him. She smelled so... sexy that her nearness was driving him crazy. He wanted to take a step back to collect himself and have her closer all at the same time.

They arrived at Thai Palace, and his stomach growled as they entered the dimly lit restaurant. A hostess seated them and left them with menus. They decided on the pad Thai and shrimp in spicy green curry and a couple of appetizers and Thai beer.

"Can we really eat that much food?" she asked as the waitress left with their orders.

"I love Thai, so yes. We can. And whatever we can't means leftovers for breakfast."

"I'm pretty much used to oatmeal for breakfast. And lots of eggs and homemade bread. But I wouldn't mind spicy curry for breakfast."

"You're up for adventure," he said. "It's why you'll have a wonderful time in the English world."

"I definitely am having a wonderful time. I love how tonight feels like a big finale but it's right at the beginning."

He nodded. "It's better that way. Have your big night out early on so you'll know if you want a repeat, or if you're more of a homebody."

"It's crazy that I don't know. Quiet nights at home under propane lamps are all I really know. My community does have get-togethers, of course, and there's lots of dating. But not to Thai restaurants. Or movies."

"Well, the Blue Gulch movie theater has two movies. One's a romantic comedy and one is heavy-duty action. Your pick."

She grinned. "Definitely the romantic comedy."

As the waitress delivered their appetizers, he wondered again if she'd go home when their time together was over. Despite the glamorous look, he could envision her in the Amish community, back in her overalls or loose, long dress and bonnet, finding her own adventure in a simple lifestyle because of how her mind worked. And he could imagine her here, in his world. What he couldn't imagine was Anna on a date with a man—in either world. Actually, he could imagine it. He just hated the thought.

"Did you look at your other three wishes?" she asked. "The ones you took from the Santa's Elves box this morning?"

"No, but they're folded up in my wallet." He pulled his wallet from the inside pocket of his jacket and smoothed the three slips of paper. "First one says, 'Dear Santa, please bring me a dump truck for Christmas. A yellow one. Thanks, Santa. You are the best! From Ethan Plotowsky, age seven.'" Colt smiled. "One yellow dump truck coming right up, Ethan Plotowsky." He put that one away and looked at the next. "'I'm looking for a volunteer to help out in the kitchen the week leading up to Christmas for Hurley's Homestyle Kitchen's annual holiday-season deliveries to county homeless shelters and soup kitchens. If you can lend a hand, just an hour, see Essie Hurley. Please leave this in the box—I can use all the volunteers I can get.' Oops," he said. "I'll drop this back in after dinner."

"Maybe we could help out," Anna said. "The twins tend to nap at around nine thirty every morning for a good hour and a half. They could nap in their strollers while we slice and dice and whatever else needs doing."

"They might be unpredictable, though," Colt said. "But we can try. I wouldn't mind learning how to make food anywhere near close as Hurley's does."

"What's the third wish?"

He put the second one away and read the last wish, and his heartstrings pulled. "It says, 'My name is Devin Lomax. I'm in sixth grade. My dad is in the army and can't come home for Christmas. He was supposed to help me get better at basketball, but I stink and didn't make the team at school. Can Santa send me a coach? My mom is a police officer and said Santa should send a coach to the Blue Gulch PD to talk to her about it. From Devin.' I was on the basketball team in middle school," Colt said. "I wouldn't mind helping the kid out."

"You have a big heart, Colt," Anna said.

"Eh, I have some free time while I'm here."

The waitress delivered their entrées, and they dug in. Colt told Anna about all the different ethnic foods he'd tried over the years. They talked so easily, Anna laughing over fumbling with her chopsticks, Colt dropping a shrimp he stole from her entrée on his lap, and he barely realized there were other people around them. To him it felt like they were the only two people in the world.

After dinner, they returned Essie's wish to the Santa's Elves box, then headed to the movie theater, and despite the film being so corny that Colt laughed twice when the scene wasn't meant to be funny, he actually enjoyed the movie and was glad the two leads finally got together in the end. As if they wouldn't!

"I wasn't so sure," Anna said as they left the theater. "You never know."

"Oh, come on. It's Hollywood. Land of the happy ending."

"Yes, but sometimes a *satisfying* ending works, too."

"I would not have been satisfied if Dirk didn't end

up with Suzannah. In fact, I would have thrown my bucket of popcorn at the screen and yelled, 'Boooo!'"

Anna laughed. "Colt Asher, you are proving yourself over and over to be a romantic."

"Me? No way. I just want my money's worth from a film. Action movie, I expect the hero to be alive at the end. Romantic comedy? The couple should be kissing and holding hands when the credits roll."

She slipped her hand into his and kissed his cheek, then burst into a grin. "Sorry, I couldn't help myself."

But she didn't let go of his hand. And he didn't pull away. He liked how her soft hand felt in his. And he liked being physically connected to her. He liked too much about this woman. *You'd better take a big step backward, Asher. You're not in this for any kind of happy ending. You're gone in a week. Don't lead her on. Don't give her expectations.*

He might be flattering himself that Anna was even interested in an older, world-weary FBI agent, but the way she looked at him sometimes, like during dinner, like now, made him well aware that she was interested. More than interested. She had feelings for him. And he'd better be damn careful with those feelings.

As it was nearing midnight and they'd be picking up the twins at six thirty, Colt suggested they head back to the inn. Anna was not disappointed. In fact, for the past hour, when they'd been having a glass of wine at the bar of a fancy restaurant, she'd wanted to say, "Let's go back to the inn and make mad, passionate love all night." Or whatever it was that people actually said. But she knew they'd end up back at the inn eventually and she'd make her move.

They tiptoed in so as not to wake the proprietor, whose apartment was also on the first floor but toward the front of the building.

"Nightcap on your patio?" she asked as they approached their hallway. Upon check-in, they'd found a bottle of wine, two wineglasses and a basket of crackers and chocolates in each of their rooms. "It's such a beautiful, special night. I can't bear for it to end."

That was the truth and it just came right out of her mouth.

He looked at her, and for a moment she was afraid he was going to say that they had to be up early in the morning and had better call it a night. She'd gotten to know this man too well. What he was really thinking was probably: *You're a virgin. Another glass of wine, lowered inhibitions, and I won't be able to control myself.*

She sure hoped not.

She had no doubt that he wanted her as bad as she wanted him. The way he'd looked at her in the bar, how his gaze had traveled every now and then to the curves of her dress...

"Anna, maybe we should call it a—"

"No, we definitely should not call it a night. I'll tell you why in your room."

He raised an eyebrow and unlocked the door.

Once inside, Anna closed the door and locked it. His eyebrow shot up again.

"I'm listening," he said.

She wasn't going to blurt out that she wanted him to make love to her. That she wanted her first time to be with him. He'd run for the hills. She'd have to show him.

She backed him up against the door and pressed against him, sliding her arms around his neck. "I've wanted to kiss you all night, Colt." She lifted her chin, her three-inch heels making her just perfect kissing height for the six-foot-plus man. She wasn't going to throw herself at him—okay, she just did, but she'd take her step back here, let him follow up her first move. If he didn't, she'd go back to her room with her tail between her legs and stare at the babies' cribs and playpens and bottles all night, reminding herself that she was the nanny and not the girlfriend.

What would he do? Walk away? Respond? He stared at her, intensity in his green eyes. Then he brought his hands up to her face and kissed her, hard and passionately, crushing her against the door. Her knees almost buckled as pure desire lit up all her nerve endings. Her hands snaked through his silky hair, and suddenly he picked her up and carried her to the bed, laying her down and covering her with his body, his mouth never leaving hers.

Her hands slid down his chest to try to unbutton his shirt. She couldn't wait to feel his naked chest against hers. But he sat up suddenly and turned toward the door.

"Anna, I won't take advantage of you."

"How are you taking advantage of me? I'm a grown woman, Colt. I'm saying yes loud and clear."

"You want a one-night stand? A three-night stand? After I bring my nephews back home, I'm gone, Anna. I've made that very clear."

Dammit. She did want it all—to have her first time be with Colt, despite knowing this wouldn't be the start of a relationship. *And* to have a relationship. To have him. Forever. Conundrum.

"I want my first time to be with you," she said before she could stop herself.

"Why?" he asked. "And I don't want you to answer that. I just want you to think about it."

"How dare you!" she snapped, scrambling off his bed. "I know my own mind, Colt Asher. Don't patronize me or condescend to me."

He stood up and crossed his arms over his chest. "Don't ask me to deflower you when you know I'll be out of your life in a few days. You think it means nothing to me to take your virginity?"

"What does it mean?" she asked.

"It means responsibility. To your feelings. How could you possibly know how you'll feel in the morning, Anna? You've never had sex before. Suddenly you're going to make love for the first time and think you can be all casual about it? Separate your feelings from the act?"

"*You* can."

He stared at her. "Exactly. And I'm not willing to take advantage of your inexperience, Anna. That's not being condescending. It's being…honorable."

She could feel steam reaching the boiling point in her ears. "Sorry I don't have a medal for you!" she said through gritted teeth and stalked to the door. She wanted to slam it so badly but the moment she saw the silver-and-white beadboard wall across the hall with the painting of a bull rider, she remembered she was at the inn with guests upstairs.

Ugh, had they all heard their argument? She'd die of embarrassment to face them at breakfast in the morning.

Oh, look, hon, there's the virgin and the man who

wouldn't have sex with her because he doesn't want the histrionics that'll surely follow.

She pulled the door closed and went into her room and locked the door, then sat at the window seat and stared out at the night.

Colt was half-right, which added to how upset she was. She didn't know how she'd feel in the morning. She didn't know if one amazing night of passion with Colt Asher would make her feel even more for him than she already did. How could it not? They'd be physically joined.

But just because she'd waited until age twenty-four to have her first time didn't mean she was waiting for her husband to be the first. She knew Colt would be out of her life in days. She'd be starting her life as an Englisher on her own. She'd date. Maybe she'd have lots of boyfriends. If she was going to have her first time, why not with a man she was madly in love with? Even if she had to say goodbye to him in a few days?

Because of everything Colt had said.

Dammit.

She got up and stood in the front of the mirror, leaning close to look at her beautiful earrings, her gift from him. She took off the dress and hung it up, kicked off her sexy shoes and removed the lacy black bra he never did see. She put on a T-shirt and yoga pants and headed into the bathroom, staring at her face in the mirror and the hint of makeup still there. Colt had kissed away the lipstick. She washed off the eyeliner and mascara and looked at herself again, hoping for some grand epiphany now that she was the same old Anna she'd always been, scrubbed clean.

But she wasn't the same old Anna.

Chapter Eleven

The next morning Anna was back in her borrowed jeans and borrowed sweater and her own lace-up boots. Colt knocked on her door at six fifteen and she gave him a quick, tight smile.

"Morning," he said.

Why did he have to look so incredibly gorgeous and sexy? He wore a navy blue henley shirt and dark jeans and cowboy boots. She blinked away the memories of him kissing her, holding her, pressing her against the door, the bed.

Speak, Anna. "Morning."

"I want to make a pit stop at the coffee shop and bring bagels and pastries to Jake's ranch as a thank-you for taking the babies all day and night. Shouldn't take too long."

"Nice idea."

No one listening to this dull, clipped conversation would have any idea that for about five minutes last night, these two people had been all over each other, kissing like it was their last day on earth, hands roaming everywhere. She almost smiled when she recalled the way Colt had picked her up and carried her to the bed, but the smile faded at the I-won't-take-advantage-of-you line.

They barely spoke at the coffee shop, except for Colt to ask what she wanted. With coffees in hand and a big box of treats and a bag of bagels with three kinds of cream cheese, they got into Colt's car. As she buckled her seat belt she was too aware of him, how close he was, the smell of his shampoo, same as hers.

"Look, Colt, before we arrive at the ranch, let's get the awkwardness out of the way so we don't act all weird in front of Jake and Emma."

He turned toward her, setting his cup in the console. "Once again, I appreciate that you say it like it is. I probably would have kept the awkwardness going."

Sigh. That was the problem.

Or was it? It wasn't like Colt hadn't acknowledged the crazy attraction between them; he'd kissed her, after all. Then he'd called things to a screeching halt because he'd also acknowledged that the aftermath would be an ugly cry-fest—on her part.

"I'm going to look you in the eye in the bright light of morning and tell you that I want you to be my first," she said. "I want you to introduce me to the wonders of sex. In a few more days we'll go our separate ways. No expectations. No tears. Just wonderful memories."

He narrowed his green eyes at her. "How do you know there won't be expectations? Or tears? On my part."

She laughed. "Is that a joke? Because it's not funny and I hate that I laughed anyway."

His smile was so beautiful that she wanted to reach out and touch his cheek. "Anna, this is new for me too. I'm an FBI agent who works alone. Suddenly I have a nanny who I feel responsible for—for many reasons. I'm not going to lie and say I don't have feelings for you. I do."

She gasped. "I knew it."

He covered her hand with his for a moment then picked up his coffee and took a sip. "I think you're amazing, Anna. And I'm obviously very attracted to you. I'm not going to just forget about you because I'm back in the field, chasing mobsters."

"So you don't want to sleep with me to protect yourself?" she asked.

"I'm just saying I think it's a bad idea for both of us. Let's just keep things on a professional level and then no one gets hurt. We go our separate ways with a clear head and good thoughts."

He was awfully focused on going his separate way. Maybe that was the problem. Maybe she had to chip away at the idea—that he had to be all lone-wolf in the first place. Why couldn't he accept his feelings for her and act on them? Why deny?

He started the ignition and pulled away so she let him focus on driving instead of the conversation. Now that she had a new tactic for reaching him, she felt less off balance. She liked having a plan.

Colt loved the Full Circle Ranch. When he'd read in CJ Morrow's initial email that his brother—their mutual brother—Jake was a successful rancher and

owned a spread in Blue Gulch, Texas, he'd been surprised that his twin was a cowboy. Colt had no idea
what he'd expected of Jake—maybe that he'd be in
law enforcement like him. Which was silly. Just because they were twins didn't mean they had anything
in common. Though from spending just a little time
with Jake, Colt saw similarities in little things.

As Colt pulled up to the ranch house, magazine-
ready with a big red barn beside it and hundreds of
acres of pasture and woodland, his twin came outside,
a baby in each arm.

Anna smiled. "I've missed those cuties."

"Me, too." He glanced at her. "And that doesn't mean
I should suddenly become a father—if that's what you
were about to say. It just means I haven't seen my baby
nephews in twenty-four hours—when I'm responsible
for them—and I'm glad to see them." He eyed Anna
to see if she accepted that or if she was giving him the
uh-huh, whatever-you-say look. He couldn't tell. She
only had eyes for Noah and Nathaniel at the moment.

Colt and Anna got out of the car and each took a
baby, smothering them with kisses and nuzzles as if it
had been weeks since they'd last seen the twins. Jake
laughed.

Colt wasn't even embarrassed. He really was going a
bit soft. "You get used to being with the babies twenty-
four/seven and an overnight away from them feels really weird."

"I know what you mean," Jake said. "Last week a
flash flood stranded me overnight on an auction trip. I
almost went out of my mind being away from Violet."

Colt smiled. "Boys give you any trouble last night?"

"They're easy and fun. We had a great time. Well,

come on in. We're actually just finishing up breakfast. We got a late start this morning. You'll meet the entire crew."

Colt and Anna followed Jake inside to the dining room. Five men and Emma, who was the ranch cook aside from being Jake's wife, were seated around the dining room table. One man immediately jumped up and got two more chairs from around a corner.

"Thanks, Golden," Jake said. "Colt, Anna, there's a playpen next to Violet's in the corner—why don't you set the boys down for a bit and have a seat and help yourself to breakfast."

"We come bearing bagels and cream cheese and pastries," Anna said, setting out the baked goods on an empty platter.

"Ooh, is that veggie cream cheese?" one of the older men asked. "Fern is after me to eat more veggies." He took a sesame bagel half and smeared it with the cream cheese.

"I don't think a teaspoon of peppers or whatever is in that counts," a younger guy said.

Jake made the introductions. The younger guy was Jake's brother, CJ. The other young man was Golden. Hank, gobbling up the sesame bagel, was the ranch foreman, and Grizzle, the oldest of the crew, was munching on a piece of bacon.

"I'm glad to finally meet you, CJ," Colt said. "It's thanks to you I'm even here."

CJ nodded and glanced from twin to twin. "You sure do look a lot alike."

"Colt is better-looking," Grizzle said on a chuckle.

"You and your wife have awfully cute twins yourself," Hank said, grabbing another bagel half and adding even more veggie cream cheese.

"Oh, we're not married," Anna said. "The babies are Colt's nephews. I'm the nanny."

All eyes to swung to Anna, then Colt.

"My sister and her husband needed emergency childcare while they went on a weeklong cruise," Colt explained. "I've never spent more than two hours with the little guys so I figured I'd need serious help."

"Enter me," Anna said.

"Well, I'm glad we have another lady present because these know-nothing guys are ganging up on me about being in the doghouse again with Fern," Hank said. "Emma here says I should apologize for saying what I meant in the wrong way, but why do I always have to apologize if I'm not wrong?"

"Tell Anna what you did to earn Fern's wrath," CJ said, shaking his head.

Hank scowled at CJ, then turned to Anna. "She asked me if her dress made her hips look big and I said yes."

There was much head shaking at the dining room table.

"Hank, every guy knows the answer to that question is always no," CJ said. "No. Plain and simple. No."

"But her hips flare out so nicely," Hank said. "Fern has one of those hourglass figures. I can't keep my eyes off her."

"And that's what you'll tell her," Emma said. "Just explain that that's what you meant."

"Why do I have to walk on eggshells with what I say?" Hank complained. "The woman knows I'm madly in love with her. Of course I love her big hips."

Anna smiled. "I agree with Emma. And maybe don't add that last part when you talk to her."

"All right, fine," Hank said. "If it's two ladies telling me."

"And four wiser men," Grizzle said.

Hank grabbed yet another bagel and sent daggers around the table, then started laughing at a joke CJ was telling. Colt glanced around the table, enjoying the camaraderie of the crew.

"So you're a traveling nanny?" CJ asked Anna. "That's interesting."

Anna laughed. "Well, I'm not a nanny by profession. I'm just helping out."

"A-ha, just as I thought," Hank said. "You're not a nanny—you're the girlfriend."

Colt was beginning to understand why Jake had referred to his foreman—in a few emails over the past several months—as needing a little refinement when it came to talking to people. He was apparently great at his job, but struck out when he opened his mouth. According to Jake, Emma had done her best operating a makeshift mealtime charm school for his ranch hands, and Hank had barely passed—just enough to get Fern to date him. But the man still kept putting his foot in his mouth.

"Well, Anna said she's helping out, so she must be," Golden said, reaching for a pastry. Colt smiled at Golden, so named for the saying about silence. Jake had mentioned that Golden was very shy and rarely spoke, but he and Emma had helped him find his voice to pursue his crush, and now they were engaged.

"Yeah," Grizzle said, also taking a pastry from the bunch that Anna and Colt had brought. Grizzle was a widower who apparently used to scare small children when he came to town because of his wild hair and long, thick straggly beard. He still had a mountain-man look, but he'd gussied up for his new love, the town's reference librarian.

"Well, if you want to know a secret," Anna said to the crew, "I'm Amish and on my *rumspringa*. Taking the job as Colt's nanny for the week he's on baby duty has been a great way for me to decide if I want to stay in the English world—meaning your world—or go back to my village and be baptized in the Amish faith."

Everyone stared at Emma.

"You're not Amish," Hank said. "Where's your bonnet?"

"When in Rome," Colt said. "She's dressed like an Englisher."

"So are you going back?" CJ asked.

"I don't know for sure yet," Anna said. "My heart is in your world. But a big piece of it is back home, with my family, with where I grew up."

Emma sipped her coffee. "Well, if you decide to stay, there are lots of nanny jobs to be had in town. I know two families looking for full-time nannies."

"Actually, I've always dreamed about becoming a nurse," Anna said. "The Amish only go to school through the eighth grade, but I have my GED. I think if I stay I'd like to go to nursing school."

Colt had a feeling this was the first time Anna had said those words aloud, the first time she'd permitted herself to express her dream as a possibility. He could absolutely see her as a nurse, dedicated to helping people.

"A friend of mine is a nurse," Emma said. "She

graduated from a nursing school in Houston. I'll email you her contact info if you'd like."

Anna beamed. "That would be great. Thank you."

Despite all the talking, plates and platters were picked clean and breakfast had wound down. It was clearly time for Jake and the crew to get to work, and Colt had taken up enough of his time. "Well, we'd better get these rascals home. Thanks again for taking care of them."

"When the crew found out we were babysitting, Grizzle read them a bedtime story," Emma said. "And Hank sang the 'Itsy Bitsy Spider' song."

"The babies really are adorable," CJ said. "My fiancée has been talking a lot about babies lately. Asking how many kids I want to have. But being around Violet and seeing how fun it is to play with your nephews has made the idea less scary."

"CJ a father. Now *that's* scary," Grizzle said with a grin, giving CJ an elbow in the ribs.

Jake laughed. "CJ will be a great dad. No doubt."

Anna scooped up Nathaniel from the playpen and Colt did the same to Noah. Jake and his brother brought out the babies' gear to Jake's car.

"Thanks again," Colt said, extending his hand.

"Anytime you need anything. I'm here."

The more time Colt spent with his twin, the closer he felt to the man. "That goes for me, too."

With everyone settled in the car, Colt waved at Jake and headed up the long dirt drive, enjoying the view of the cattle and horses and sheep in various pastures. Jake had a very different life than Colt did, and he'd like to spend more time at the ranch. Maybe when he was done with his next case, he could come back and have some time with Jake and Sarah, as well. He'd like to hear more about her and how he and Jake had come into the world.

Huh. He'd never really wondered about that before. But now he was curious about her story and who his biological father was. Jake had relayed the information that their birth father had turned his back on Sarah and denied he was the father and that Sarah's mother had sent her to a home for pregnant teenagers. He hadn't spent much time letting any of that penetrate because it seemed so personal and he wasn't sure he wanted to get too close to Sarah Mack Ford.

But he felt his interest expanding. He was…changing. And he wondered if the beautiful woman in the passenger seat had something to do with that.

"Maybe before we leave for Houston we can drop by the ranch again," Anna said as Colt turned onto Blue Gulch Street and stopped for a red light. "I'd love to visit the livestock."

"I'm sure that can be arranged."

It would give Colt a nice reason to come back, she realized, if he felt as though he needed one. She knew he'd like to spend some more time with the Morrows before he left the area.

"Great group of guys," Anna said. "Emma must have to do a lot of refereeing with that crew."

Colt smiled. "I'll bet."

"I'll look forward to getting the contact info from her friend," Anna said. "I'm not sure of what the future will hold for me, but I do want to explore the idea of nursing school and see if it's possible for me."

"Of course it's possible. You can do anything you want."

Anna felt her heart ping. "Well, I don't know the first thing about applying to college or what that's all about. Maybe my background won't be enough to meet the application requirements."

"And maybe it will," he said. "In fact, I'm sure it will. You have a very interesting life story, Anna Miller. And you do have your GED."

"Me, a college student. With the goal of becoming a nurse." Excitement and butterflies flew around her midsection. She felt tears sting her eyes even though she had a dopey—no, proud—smile on her face. She *could* do this. "And Houston would be just the right place. A big city like I'd always dreamed of and just fifteen minutes from my family. And right next door to Grass Creek. I could visit the Amish market for a taste of home anytime I needed to."

"And you could run into me now and again," he said.

Every muscle in her body twitched. "Now and again, huh?"

"Well, in the coffee shop, the dry cleaner, the grocery store. We'll be neighbors."

Her smile faded. Oh, Colt. For a minute there, she forgot he was halfway gone already—in his mind, anyway. She'd forgotten all about her plan to make him see that he could have his job and love, his work and a serious relationship. A wife. Children.

How exactly she was going to make him see this, she had no clue. But she had a few more days.

He had her heart. There was no denying that. And she also knew that staying in the English world wasn't dependent on whether Colt wanted her in his life or not.

She was staying, regardless.

Oh, God. There it was. She was staying.

"I'm staying, Colt. I'm staying in your world. I kept telling myself I wasn't a hundred-percent sure, but I think I've known all along. And I know now. For sure. I'm staying."

"Welcome," he said, giving her a smile that stopped her heart.

"I'm going to become a nurse. And in my free time I'm going to volunteer the way my cousin Mara does, helping those in need. I'm sure there are clinics that need volunteer nurses."

"I'm very impressed by you, Anna. You know what you want and you go for it. That's how it's done."

She beamed. And thought, *yes, yes it is, Colt Asher. And I also want you.*

Chapter Twelve

The next day, the babies were up early and it was another warm morning at almost sixty degrees, so Anna took Noah and Nathaniel out for an early stroll after breakfast. When the town began to wake up she treated herself to a mocha latte at the coffee shop, then stopped in at Hurley's Homestyle since there was a light on in the kitchen.

An older woman answered the doorbell. "Hi, there," she said. "I'm Essie Hurley. I've seen you in here before, I'm pretty sure."

"Yes. I had an amazing lunch here. My first barbecued po'boy. My name is Anna Miller, and I'm here in town temporarily—as nanny to these cuties—until Christmas Eve. I took a couple of wishes from the Santa's Elves box and my boss and I would both like to volunteer in the kitchen."

"Oh, great!" Essie said. "I see you've got the babies with you, but my granddaughters have babies and there are playpens full of fun toys in the kitchen if you'd like to commit to an hour now."

Anna smiled. "I'd love it. I'll just text my boss. We're staying just a few doors down at the inn."

After shooting off a quick text to Colt, Anna took Noah out of the stroller while Essie plucked Nathaniel, and they headed inside. The kitchen was big and country-style, and there were a few cooks already at work.

"Everyone, this is Anna Miller. She's our Santa's Elf helper for the Christmas-week food donations."

Essie made the introductions. All three of Essie's granddaughters, Annabel, Georgia and Clementine, were in the kitchen. Annabel had a five-year-old step-daughter and a baby. Georgia's baby was almost the same age as Annabel's, and Clementine had a nine-year-old and was helping to raise her husband's young orphaned nephews. "Let's set down your little guys right here," she said, putting Nathaniel in the empty playpen next to the one that two other babies were sharing. Anna placed Noah beside him, and they both immediately reached for the colorful baby toys in the pen. There were a few toys that hung up on the insides as well, so that they could stand and stretch their legs and cruise around the sides.

With the twins settled, Anna put on an apron and stood next to Essie at a counter by the window. Her job was to scoop Essie's homemade spicy coleslaw into small containers with lids and place them into boxes that would be delivered to area food banks.

"I love these silly quizzes," Annabel said with a

smile, her long auburn hair in a low ponytail. She had a magazine open at her station, where she was stirring the contents of a big silver pot. If Anna wasn't mistaken, she smelled the delicious aroma of sweet, tangy barbecue sauce. "'How to know if your man really loves you. Christmas is coming and you hint that you'd love to go away for a preseason getaway. He, *A*, pretends he doesn't hear you, *B*, avoids you, or *C*, whisks you off for a surprise adventure at the place of your dreams.'"

"I think your guy can still love you and pretend not to hear you about a preseason getaway," Clementine said. "I mean, who isn't really busy right before Christmas? Who has time to go away? I've got a daughter and two little boys to take care of, a husband, a home, extended family and work. I'm going away with 'my man' for a weekend?"

Georgia laughed. "You do need a vacation, Clem. I say if your man loves you, he doesn't pretend he doesn't hear you, he doesn't avoid you, and he surprises you with the getaway after Christmas when life is back to normal."

"Agreed," Essie says.

"What do you think, Anna?" Clementine asked.

"Me? I'm the last person to ask about relationships. I've never even had a real relationship. I mean, I tried to date here and there, and I almost started dating someone who was my best friend, but I just didn't feel what you're supposed to feel, what I think you're supposed to feel. Until now," she added, frowning.

"You're in love with someone!" Annabel said. "Does he know?"

"I've been pretty open about it," she said. "But I

haven't come right out and said 'I love you' to him. He'd run for the hills."

Georgia laughed. "Or not. Sometimes you have to just tell a man like it is. Honestly, they can be a little slow on the uptake when it comes to romance. My husband had no idea I was madly in love with him."

"Really?" Anna asked. "So you think I should just tell him?"

"Well, let's get your answer to the quiz question about him," Clementine said. "Then we'll advise you."

"He might pretend he didn't hear me say I wanted a getaway," Anna said, capping another container of coleslaw. He'd done that a few times. "He might avoid me." He'd done that before, too. "But—" Anna froze.

"But what?" Essie asked.

Anna told them the story of how she and Colt met—the stolen guinea pig, Colt driving into her Amish village with his FBI badge and how he'd come back to hire her as his nanny.

"He did listen to me. He'd heard every word I said about not having a chance to go on my *rumspringa*, to experience life in the English world. Yes, he needed a nanny, but I'm sure an Amish stranger wasn't his only option. He took me on the ultimate preseason getaway because he heard me loud and clear."

"He loves you," Annabel said.

Georgia paused with her rolling pin in the air. "Yup. He loves you."

Clementine nodded. "True love."

Anna laughed and shook her head. "True love before he even really knew me? We'd had one ten-minute conversation before he hired me."

"Love at first sight. It happens. Clem fell for Logan the first time she saw him."

"I did. A few minutes after I talked to him I thought, I'm gonna marry that man. And I did. Took a while to get us there, but it happened," she said, holding up her left hand, where a gold band shone in the early morning light.

"Sometimes, you just know about a person," Essie said.

Colt loved her? After meeting her in *Daed's* overalls and smelling of baby goat? No. No way. He'd had a need for a nanny. He'd just met her right before the issue came up. He'd wisely realized they could help each other out. That was all there was to that.

"Well, if a man loves you, there would be no obstacles for him, right?" Anna asked, scooping the coleslaw into the cups. She was getting faster at this. "I mean, let's say he was a lone-wolf type who was completely focused on his job and had no time or interest in having a family."

"You've met my husband, detective Nick Slater?" Georgia said, smiling.

"He was the same way?" Anna asked.

"Exactly the same way. Sometimes a man can be madly in love and scared to death of it, unwilling to let himself feel that much for a woman."

"But it shouldn't be so hard, right?" Anna said. Isn't that what Caleb had said? That their love was so easy, so natural, and romance wasn't supposed to be about arguments and stomping off. *Stop confusing crazy emotional tantrums for passion and love*, he'd said, and Anna had spent days trying to figure out if that was what she was doing. If that was what she was still doing.

"Sometimes it's not hard at all," Essie said. "I was married for almost forty years to a wonderful man. Love at first sight for both of us. Nothing hard about it. And I'll tell you, we were plenty passionate. But the last few months I've had myself a beau and he's a different man and we're different people. There are times when it feels like I've known him forever and other times when it's like he's from Mars."

Anna laughed. "That's how it feels with Colt. And I think he feels that same way about me."

"Well, if you love him, if he's the one, don't let anything interfere with telling him," Annabel said. "I lost several years with West when we were younger because he thought he wasn't good enough for me, and I didn't realize I needed to conk him over the head with how I felt about him."

"And I don't have a lot of time," Anna said. "We're leaving on Christmas Eve morning to return his nephews to his sister and her husband. My job will be over. My reason for being with Colt will be over. And he intends to start working immediately on a big case. That'll be that."

"So get your man," Clementine said. "From everything you've said, there's no way he'll let you get away."

Anna wasn't so sure of that herself. Colt equally wanted two things, it seemed. To have Anna. And to get away from Anna.

Only one would win out.

"Georgia, how did your husband realize that he didn't have to be a lone wolf?" Anna asked. "That he could have love and family, too. Was it something you helped with?"

The baker kneaded the dough, adding a sprinkle of flour. "I tried. Hard. I was pregnant with his baby at the time, too, and he was still very tough to convince that he had what it took to be a good father and husband. He had to see it for himself. He had to believe it. And he eventually did, but I did push the issue. I wasn't going to let him walk away without putting my all into saving us."

"But how?" Anna asked. "I want to show him that he can have his job and a life outside of it. But how?"

"Just be you," Essie said. "Just be there. That's how."

Georgia nodded. "It's Colt who has to do the rest."

Anna stacked her many containers of spicy coleslaw in a box and taped it up, then carried it to the walk-in fridge, the blast of air barely registering since a chill had already crept inside her. What if Colt didn't, couldn't—*wouldn't*—do the rest?

The twins were cranky after their morning nap, so Colt and Anna had stayed at the inn for a few hours, watching old movies and newer ones, ordering in every kind of food that Blue Gulch offered, from Chinese to Indian to Italian. They borrowed board games from the inn's proprietor and Anna played Monopoly and Sorry for the first time. Colt taught her how to play poker, but she didn't have much of a poker face and gave herself away every hand. Nathaniel peed on Colt's favorite T-shirt during a changing session, and Noah threw up on Anna after she'd cautiously tried offering him Cheerios once his tummy bug seemed gone. Colt had never spent time like this with a woman who wasn't his sister. When it was clear the boys were well enough to go out for some fresh air, Colt almost missed Anna's room at the inn, the constant playing and singing of lullabies.

And it was time to make sure Colt fulfilled the wishes he'd taken from the Santa's Elves box on Hurley's porch. Anna held the door as he wheeled the stroller into Blue Gulch toys, on a mission for everything on his list. Anna went one way and he went another, hoping to find Brady Canby's snow globe for his sister. The store was crowded; it was just days before Christmas, and he hoped he didn't wait too long.

Nope, he hadn't. There, right between a snow globe with Mr. and Mrs. Claus and one with Santa's reindeer, was a ballerina snow globe. She was atop a Christmas tree, colorful gifts at the bottom, a tall nutcracker standing sentry.

"I found the perfect snow globe for Brady," Colt called, waving Anna over. He thought of Brady Canby, eleven years old, already cynical about Santa. As Colt had been as a kid. When Colt was ten, he'd accidentally knocked his sister's porcelain doll, her favorite doll, a gift from their grandparents, off her dresser with a bat he'd been swinging, as he'd been showing off his baseball moves in her room, despite her yelling at him to get out. The more she told him to leave, the more he swung the bat. And then…smash.

She'd sobbed, he'd gotten into big trouble, sent to his room, no TV for a week, and he'd had a list of extra chores to earn back the thirty-five dollars the doll had cost. The night he'd broken the doll, he'd gone into Cathy's room to apologize, and at first she'd told him to beat it, then had softened when she saw how upset he really was. "Sorry about what Daddy said to you," she'd said, and to this day he could remember the shame he'd felt.

His father had said, "You're such a screwup. How'd I get such a screwup for a kid?" Colt had been afraid he'd get a hard sock in the arm, but his father had just shaken his head and walked away.

Colt *had* messed up a lot as a kid. Some bad grades, particularly on spelling tests. Some school-yard fights, a baseball or two through neighbors' windows. He'd insulted a neighbor's daughter when they were teenagers without meaning to and she'd gone off crying. It had been weeks before he'd heard the end of that. For a long time Colt had tried to figure out how to earn his father's respect, but nothing had worked. Not A's on his report card or the right girlfriends or how he dressed. The only thing that had gotten his father's attention was when Colt said he planned to also become an FBI agent. He wanted to be like his father. He had no idea what an FBI agent even did or how it was different than being a cop. His father seemed to like the notion of Colt following in his footsteps, but they'd never gotten close. Henry Asher was a distant man and there was no bridge to reach him. "People are just who they are," his mother would say when his sister would complain that Daddy didn't come to her school concert or seem to care that she won an award.

And Colt was just who he was. A lone wolf. Except lately he didn't want to be. The thought of returning to Houston and going his separate way from Anna was hard to imagine. He liked being around her. He liked being with her. He liked seeing her first thing in the morning, last thing at night. The absence of her would be noticeable.

His life had changed so much in these days that Anna had been part of. He was more open to a relationship with his birth relatives. And suddenly he was imagining Anna still in his life when the week was up.

Anna came over to where he stood, smiling at the row of snow globes on the shelves. "Aww, that snow globe is definitely perfect," she said, examining it from all angles. "I love the nutcracker by the Christmas tree." She tilted up the bottom and twisted the prong. "Dance of the Sugar Plum Fairy" began playing and the ballerina twirled atop the tree.

Colt turned it right-side up and snow began falling. "One ballerina snow globe—check. But I'd also like to get Brady something for himself, too."

"What would an eleven-year-old boy like?" she asked as they began looking through the aisles.

"I would have wanted this," he said, picking up a cool-looking skateboard. Below was a row of helmets and safety gear. He chose a navy helmet and took a pack of the safety gear, too.

"Very kind of you, Colt. We can check Brady Canby off the list. Essie said we can drop off all Santa's Elves gifts at Hurley's and put them under the Christmas tree with name tags, and she'd call the recipients to alert them to pick up their gifts."

"She's really doing a nice thing," Colt said. "Makes me want to volunteer in the kitchen even more. I didn't have a chance to get over there."

She picked up a cartoon lunch box and bit her lip. "Uh, Colt? When I volunteered there this morning, your name might have come up in conversation."

"My name? Why?"

"Well, one of the Hurley sisters was taking a magazine quiz about romance, and they were answering a question about the men in their lives, and you're kind of the man in mine. Unromantically speaking, of course."

He raised an eyebrow. "What was the question?"

"If I hinted I wanted to go away on a pre-Christmas getaway, would you pretend you didn't hear, avoid me or whisk me away?"

The green eyes narrowed at her. "What did you say I would do?"

"At first I didn't think such a question could apply to me. But then I realized you not only did hear me and didn't avoid me, but you did whisk me away. Here I am."

"Babysitting two seven-month-olds round-the-clock for a week is hardly a Christmas getaway."

"Oh, it is," she said. "It certainly is. If you're me."

He smiled. "I passed the test. I figured I'd get the low score in any love quiz. Zero to ten points—dump this Neanderthal immediately."

Anna laughed. "The opposite."

He gave a tight smile and moved on down the aisle. He didn't want to talk about himself. Or them—where romance was concerned. Luckily they were in a toy store on a mission and he had a good excuse for changing the subject. "Here's the sporting goods. This is a pretty decent basketball. I'll pick this up for the boy whose dad is overseas. After we're done here, I'll call his mom at the police station and talk to her about arranging a couple of games before we leave."

Anna nodded. "And there's your yellow dump truck for Ethan Plotowsky," she said, reading through the wishes. "I delivered the doll for Sophie to Hurley's already, and I called the company Jake recommended to patch Amanda Lottertin's roof, so I'm all set. Now that you've got the truck, you are, too."

"Let's go pick more wishes," Colt said after he paid and was laden with bags. "I could do this all day."

"You *are* a softy."

"Everyone should have a good Christmas."

Anna flung her arms around him and hugged him tight, and after his initial surprise, he put down his bags and hugged her back.

"What was that for?" he asked.

"I just think you're awesome."

He smiled. "I'm not that awesome. Trust me."

"Nope," she said. "Although I do trust you in every other sense."

"Let's go raid the wishes box. We'll each pick one more."

Colt, a Santa's elf. He was surprising himself more every day. Next thing he knew he'd be proposing to Anna. He chuckled to himself, then sobered. Fast.

Where the hell had that come from?

Back in her room, the twins settled for their naps, Anna reread the email that Emma Morrow had forwarded from her friend the nurse. There were links to a university in Houston and the nursing program. She texted Colt to ask if he'd hang out with the twins while she used the inn's desktop computer in the parlor to look up the university and check out the program and download an application. In thirty seconds he was in her room and she was overcome with the urge to kiss him. To be in his arms again. To be the object of his desire, as he was for her. When she'd impulsively hugged him in the toy store, he'd hugged her back tight for a moment—a real hug with affection, with longing.

What was between them, under the surface, was very real. And if she was going to get her man as the Hurley sisters advised, she would have to tell him how she felt.

All she had to say was "I love you, Colt Asher. I love you and want to be with you. Forever." She didn't have to say that last lone-wolf-scaring bit. Just the first two parts.

"Colt?"

"Hmm?" he asked, sitting down at her desk chair.

"I have something to tell you."

"Okay." He stood up, and she could tell he was bracing himself.

"I want to say this in the cold light of day. When we're just standing around, living our lives, going about our business. Not during a romantic moment, like a kiss you'll say was a mistake afterward."

He stared at her, waiting.

"I'm going to use the computer in the parlor. But before I go, I want you to know that I'm in love with you. I want to be with you. That is all."

"Oh, that's all?" he said, quirking a smile that faded. He closed his eyes. "Forget I said that. You caught me off guard."

"In a bad way?"

"There's really only one way to catch someone off guard," he said.

Ouch. She tried for a neutral expression. "Right. Well, now you know how I feel. I said it. It's out there." She headed to the door. "I don't expect you to say anything now, Colt. I just wanted you to know." She could feel her cheeks flaming. "Okay, so 'bye."

She quickly opened the door and ran out, her heart pounding.

Colt dropped back down on the chair, the air knocked out of him. She loved him?

He knew he'd been right not to take her up on her offer to be her first lover. It wasn't about sex and experience for Anna. It was about love.

There was a piece of him that felt all gooey and warm. A great woman was in love with him. He was honored, actually.

But a bigger piece of him was already shuttering up like a hurricane was approaching.

He was still sitting at the desk, staring into space, when Anna returned, waving a few sheets of paper.

She was beaming. "I downloaded the application for nursing school in Houston!"

"I have no doubt you'll get in, Anna. You're going to be a great nurse."

She smiled and glanced at the papers in her hand. "Oh, the boys are still sleeping. I'll stay with them now. I'm going to start filling out my application. We can meet for dinner later."

He loved how passionate she was about nursing school. Every day, every hour, he learned more about her and was more and more impressed by the person she was.

"Anna, I wanted to get back to our conversation before you left. I don't want to just pretend I didn't hear you or that I'm avoiding you."

She laughed, but then her smiled faded and she put

down the application. "So you're choosing *C*, you're going to tell me you love me, too, and that we have a future together?"

"I—" He didn't know what he wanted to say. He didn't know what he wanted. "I just know that I care very much about you."

"That's not one of the multiple-choice options."

He ran a hand through his hair, not sure what to say. The last thing he wanted to do was hurt her. "Then how about I just say the truth, Anna. That meeting you wasn't in my plans. Suddenly, you're the biggest thing in my life."

"Guess you'll have to go with it, then." She smiled, but it didn't reach her eyes. "Look, I know you're meeting Devin Lomax behind the police station in ten minutes, so let's just save this conversation for when we have more time."

"Meet you back here for dinner?" Not that he'd have more to add by then.

She nodded. "How about seven? We could probably both use some real time apart to think."

He nodded. He didn't like the idea of spending the next few hours without her. Especially because he'd soon be saying goodbye.

He froze. So was that how it was? He would be saying goodbye? That had come out of him unbidden. Because he was so programmed to feel that way? Or because he wanted to go back into the field, to have ridding Texas of organized crime the only burn in his gut?

"See you at seven," he said. "Later, little guys," he added, glancing at the napping Noah and Nathaniel.

He left quietly, missing them all the moment he closed the door behind him.

* * *

"I'm looking for Devin Lomax's mother," Colt said to the receptionist at the Blue Gulch Police Department.

"First desk on the left," the receptionist said. "You can't miss her since she's the only female officer right now."

Colt walked over to Lynne Lomax's desk, carrying the basketball with a big red-and-green bow on it. Lynne was in her late thirties with short blond hair and a warm smile. "Hi, I'm Colt Asher. I called earlier about the wish your son put in the Santa's Elves box at Hurley's."

She smiled at the basketball. "I appreciate that—and that you're taking time from your vacation to give him some tips and show him some moves," Lynn said. "I did a background check to make sure you're who you say you are."

"Wouldn't have it any other way," he said.

"Devin is out back now, working on his free throws. He knows you're coming."

Colt headed outside. Devin Lomax was a short, skinny eleven-year-old in a T-shirt and athletic pants. He had brown wavy hair and hazel eyes and his expression said: *whatever.*

"Hey, Devin, I'm Colt. Santa's Elf. Merry Christmas." He bounced the ball over to him.

"You don't look like an elf," the boy said, raising an eyebrow. He took off the bow and stuck it to the front of his shirt, then dribbled his new ball.

"Elves come in all shapes and sizes."

"But can they shoot?" the boy asked, throwing a

three-pointer…and missing. He sighed and hung his head. "I stink. I'm never going to make the team."

"You can make the team by doing three things, Devin. The first is believing that you *will* make the team."

"Why should I believe it when it's obviously not going to happen? I can't even get the ball in the hoop."

"Because you don't think you can. Believing in yourself is key. You want to aim that ball and think 'It's going in. I can do it.' And you've got to feel it."

The eyebrow went up again. "Okay. You said there were three things."

"Second, keep your eye on the hoop. Feel the distance between the ball in your hand and the hoop. Feel it. Then aim, your eye on the hoop."

"Feel it. Aim. Eye on the hoop. What's the third thing?"

"Fun," Colt said, stealing the ball and dribbling it to the hoop, then slam-dunking it in. "Yes! Asher scores!"

"Fun for you, maybe," Devin said with a grin.

Colt bounced the ball over to him. "Okay, show me your free throw, remembering what I told you."

"The ball is going in," Devin said. "Hoop, I feel you. Aim with my eyes on the hoop." He shot—and missed. "Told you I stink."

"You missed because you forgot the third thing—to have fun. Basketball is pure pleasure. Not frustration. Even the best of the NBA stars miss."

"I guess. My dad never misses a free throw. Sinks it every time."

"You miss him a lot, huh," Colt said.

Devin dribbled and walked toward the hoop, wiping at his eyes, and Colt knew he was crying. His heart squeezed for the kid.

"Are you trying to make the team to please your dad?" he asked, hoping that wasn't the case.

"My dad was on the basketball team in middle school and high school. He's even on his squadron team when they have downtime. I want to be like him, but he can't help me get better because he's not here."

"I know what you mean. I always wanted to be like my dad. I became an FBI agent because my dad was an agent. I wanted to be like him."

"And now you are."

"Actually, I'm not," Colt admitted. He froze, the words echoing in his head. "I mean, I'm an agent and I love my job. But my dad and I are very different people. He wasn't an athlete at all in school, but I was. My favorite sport is baseball, but his is hockey. He doesn't even like baseball."

"Want to know a secret?" Devin asked.

"Sure."

"I don't like basketball. I just wanted to get good at it so my dad would be proud of me when he comes home."

"Is he proud of you about other things?"

"My grades. I'm second smartest in my class. And class president."

Colt smiled. "You don't have to be everything your dad is. You just have to be you. Do what you want to do, what makes you happiest. Maybe that's learning to shoot hoops, but maybe it's not. Maybe you're meant to put all your energy into being the greatest class president. Maybe you prefer chess to basketball."

"I do, actually. But my dad thinks it's really boring. My mom likes to play with me, though."

"Sounds like you have a great family, Devin."

"So you don't think my dad would be disappointed if I don't try out for the team again?"

"I don't think it would even cross his mind. I'll bet he just wants you to be happy. That's what makes a dad happy."

"Can you play chess?"

"I'm not great, but yeah, I can play."

"Can I still keep the ball you got me even though it might gather dust in my closet?"

"Absolutely."

"My mom has a chess set in her desk. I can go get it and we can play out here on the picnic table."

"Sounds like a plan."

Devin grinned and ran toward the back door, then turned back. "Thanks for the ball! Did I say that?"

Colt smiled. "You just did."

Devin ran into the station, and Colt watched through the bars on the window as the boy talked to his mom, and then they hugged, his mother looking very relieved. She turned and saw him watching and mouthed *Thank you*. Colt held up a hand and smiled.

He hadn't expected his meeting with Devin to go like this. He hadn't expected a lot of what had happened his week.

He stared up at the hoop, remembering playing by himself for hours in the school yard. His dad was never interested in playing with him when he was around, which wasn't often. It hadn't occurred to Colt before that he wouldn't be like his father, that all households weren't run like this. He could be a really good dad for all he knew. Fatherhood was about commitment and love and being there and seeing your kid for who he was instead of who you wanted him to be.

But Devin Lomax wasn't his kid. His nephews weren't his kids. Maybe it was easy to think you knew it all when you weren't the one in the trenches 24/7—for real. He was just a side-seat parent to his nephews. Anna was the real force these past several days.

So maybe he'd be distant like his father was if he had his own son or daughter. Maybe if Devin was his son, their conversation would be very different. How could he know for sure?

He thought of Anna, knowing absolutely nothing for sure because everything was so new. But she was as sure as can be of staying in his world. With or without him.

Courage score for FBI agent: zero. Amish woman: he'd lost count of the number, but it was high.

The most important question: was he really going to walk away from her in two days?

How could he? Because as he waited for Devin Lomax to come out with the chess set, he envisioned Anna Miller holding a little Anna or a little Colt in her arms. His baby.

Why the hell didn't he know his own mind? Did he love the woman or not? His heart said yes. Screamed yes.

But his head said no.

Which one was right?

Chapter Thirteen

Anna had no idea how Colt was going to react when he walked into her room. The lights were dimmed. His nephews were once again at his twin's house for the night. And Anna was practically naked in her bed. Waiting.

Yes, this was an ambush.

She wasn't all that naked. But she was wearing a sexy nightie she'd bought in a boutique today. She'd come out and run into Emma Morrow, Jake's wife, with baby Violet, and they'd all spent a couple of hours together. Emma had asked what Anna had bought in the boutique, and when Anna pulled out the sexy black nightie and explained she was trying to seduce a man who wouldn't be seduced, Emma insisted on taking the twins home so that Anna could set the stage.

He'd said no to sex. But on their penultimate night together, she had a new plan.

After meeting Devin, he'd spent an hour helping out in Hurley's kitchen and then delivering the boxes of food to area food banks and shelters. A half hour ago, he'd texted her that he was back at the inn, about to take a long, hot shower, and would knock on her door to see about dinner plans in about fifteen minutes.

She'd be waiting.

The knock came. Anna got up and glanced at herself in the mirror, her hair loose around her shoulders, the scrap of lace on her body showing everything she had. Only the lamp on the desk was on, dimly illuminating the room.

She sucked in a breath, took a Zen moment to collect herself and opened the door.

Colt stared at her, his gaze dropping from her face to her sexy outfit. "Expecting someone?"

She laughed. "You're not supposed to make jokes at a time like this."

His expression was dead serious now. "A time like what?"

She took his hand and pulled him into the room, then locked the door. "The twins and I spent some time with Emma and Violet. I ran into her in town. She insisted on taking Noah and Nathaniel home with her, and I had plans for you tonight, so I hope that's all right with you."

"That the twins are at Jake's or your plans for me?"

"Both."

"Depends what you have in mind," he said, staring at her.

"I've asked you to be my first. You thought that was a bad idea. I flat out told you earlier that I'm in love with you. You said nothing. Which is fine—I told you to think on it. Whether we're together or not, Colt, I want my first time to be with you. I'm in love with you and I'll never have another *rumspringa*. This is it. I want you to make love to me. If you're out of my life in two days, I'll still have my memories. And I want this to be part of those memories."

He closed his eyes for a moment and then took both her hands in his. "I don't want to hurt you, Anna. Can't you understand that? Casual sex isn't your thing. Trust me."

"I'm sure it's not. But there's nothing casual about this for me. I'll be making love with the man I love. Knowing full well he'll be out of my life in a couple of days. But this is what I want. Tonight has nothing to do with whether we have a future. Tonight is about tonight. Only tonight."

He held her gaze, and she could see the intensity there. He wanted her, but he was about to force himself to leave. *Please don't walk out*, she prayed silently.

"You're *sure*, Anna? One-hundred-percent sure?"

Relief. He wasn't going anywhere. Tonight, anyway. "I'm sure," she said, reaching out to unbutton his shirt. He didn't stop her.

She took off his shirt, her hands splaying on his muscular chest, then moving up to his broad shoulders and his face. She lifted up her chin and kissed him, and he took her in his arms and backed her against the door, his mouth exploring hers, his hands running over the lacy satin negligee. And then finally, both hands slipped underneath, his large warm hands on her bare skin, her waist and upward to her breasts, where he lingered. His hands moved back down, caressing her hips, and then he froze.

"Something wrong?" she teased on a whisper in his ear.

He gulped in a breath. "No underwear."

"Nope," she said, pulling him closer and undoing his belt buckle and lowering the zipper.

She watched him step out of his sexy jeans, the black boxer briefs making him look like an underwear model. With her gaze on his, she slid those down and then wrapped her hand around his erection. She'd been worried when she got to this point that she'd have no idea what to do. She'd never gone this far before. But Colt seemed to like what she was doing just fine. He growled and kissed her neck, then nipped aside the lacy material to kiss her breasts.

Suddenly he picked her up and carried her to the bed, laid her down and began kissing every inch of her body.

"You'll be needing this," she said, reaching into the drawer on the bedside table for the box of condoms she bought from the drugstore earlier this afternoon. She hadn't been embarrassed or blushed. She'd marched up the counter and said, "Just this, please" and was thrilled with her little plastic bag when she walked out.

"The whole box?" he asked with a smile.

"Maybe," she whispered, kissing his neck, his shoulders, his glorious chest.

And just a few moments later, everything she'd ever heard about sex, in whispers and hushes, everything she'd read about in books and magazines, she now knew was true.

And if she had her way, he *would* be going through that entire box. Because this might be her first and last time with the man she loved more than anything in this world.

* * *

Colt watched Anna sleep and brushed back her hair from her beautiful face, unable to stop staring at her. *I love you, too*, he whispered silently. But he wasn't ready to say the words aloud. He could hear them inside his head, his heart, his gut, quietly though, like all his nerve endings were whispering in a chant: *I love you, Anna Miller*. He'd been hearing those whispers for days now but had ignored them. Now he couldn't.

So what now? This beautiful butterfly was going to fit into his gloomy world back in Houston, where he never could be sure if he'd come home in one piece? When Colt was undercover, he was weeks in the field and there would be spotty communication, if any. Could she deal with that?

God, Colt, the woman barely used a telephone or electricity for twenty-four years. She's not exactly used to constant communication anyway.

But still. She wasn't used to people she loved being in dangerous situations. And he wasn't used to having someone to care about while in those dangerous situations. What if his feelings for Anna made him hold back on the job? He couldn't afford that.

The one thing he did know was that he didn't have a con woman on his hands. Colt had figured it would be a long time before he'd trust another woman after what had happened with Jocelyn—discovering the woman he thought could finally be the one turning out to be a criminal. A high-level drug dealer. Sickening.

This amazing Amish woman sleeping next to him managed to banish Jocelyn from all the dark recesses of his mind and heart. No easy feat.

Everything about Anna was pure openness. He

trusted her. And because he could trust her, he could love her.

He just wasn't so sure if loving her was the best thing *for* her. She didn't know what having an FBI special agent was all about. For the past several days, she'd had him all to herself, on vacation in this quaint town, playing family. Back home in Houston, he'd leave every morning with a gun in his holster. Some mornings he'd wake up undercover in the field. Could she deal with that, the danger, the not knowing? Did he want to put her through that? She was just starting out her life, applying to nursing school, discovering who she was outside of her village.

He wasn't sure. It wasn't fair of him to speak for her, to make decisions for her. That wasn't how you treated someone you loved and respected.

His heart heavy, he turned away, trying to figure this out from his end, not hers. But she was wrapped up in every thought he had.

His phone pinged with a text and Colt carefully got out of bed, not wanting to wake Anna. He grabbed the phone off the desk. Harlan.

I need you back 12/26, first thing. Time to infiltrate/ undercover. Attached is the intel on Duvall.

Well, it looked like Anna was going to find out sooner than he thought if she could handle having an FBI agent for a boyfriend.

When Anna woke up, a warm, gooey feeling of pure happiness burst inside her, despite the fact that, as she opened her eyes, she was sure Colt Asher would not be in bed beside her.

But he was.

"You're here," she said.

"Of course I am."

Of course I am. No. Nothing he'd said in the past week indicated that he would be there the morning after.

"Anna," he said, putting his arm around her. "No matter what happens between us when we get back to Houston, I'd never disappear on you. I'd never leave you wondering. If I can't be with you, I'll tell you. As I have."

"But you have told me. That's why I thought you'd be out jogging at six a.m."

He smiled. "Touché. But last night was a game changer. I knew it would be for me, Anna. It's probably why it was so easy to say no to sex before. Because I knew once I touched you, I wouldn't be able to let you go."

"So you're not letting me go?"

"That depends on you. I got a text from my boss this morning. Harlan needs me back the day after Christmas. First thing. I'm going undercover in the Duvall crime syndicate. I could be gone for a week, two weeks—I won't be able to say. Can you deal with the uncertainty of that?"

"If you can, I can," she said.

"Jesus, Anna, how the hell do you know?"

"If you're willing to risk your life to protect the people of Houston, of Texas, from a monster criminal who thinks nothing of soliciting children to sell drugs, who kidnaps prostitutes and turns them into trafficked victims, who murders without a thought, then I need to support you, not cause you stress about your life's calling, Colt."

He stared at her. "How does an Amish woman know about Duvall? About human trafficking and drugs?"

"An Amish woman who read newspapers every day in Grass Creek before and after market time. Yes, I lived a sheltered life. But my heart, mind and soul have always been out here. What I read in the newspapers didn't make me want to stay in my village, cocooned. It made me want to be here, finding my own calling, helping. I'm going to be a trauma nurse, Colt."

He was still staring at her, and she had the feeling he wanted to say something but was holding back.

"You're something else, Anna Miller," he finally said, pulling her into his arms.

She waited for him to tell her he loved her, that they'd have a life together once they returned to Houston. She waited five minutes. Then ten. But he was silent, just holding her, stroking her back, caressing her hair.

"We'd better go get Noah and Nathaniel," he said, then kissed her cheek and got out of bed.

He loved her. She knew it. He was ruminating, letting everything sink in, particularly this new information that she actually had a clue about the work he did, that she could handle it. That she was tougher than she appeared. Colt had probably been counting on her not handling it, making it easier for him to walk away to shield himself.

She smiled. Not happening. He was hers and she was his. She'd let him have his time to digest. But she believed deep inside that she and Colt would be together. They *had* to be.

* * *

Colt and Anna spent a couple of hours at Jake's ranch, Anna going off with Emma to see the animals, and Jake and Colt walking the property with the babies. Colt was amused at how Jake's big orange cat, aptly named Redford, trailed them around the property. And he was glad to hear that Hank, the Full Circle's foreman, had indeed apologized to his on-and-off girlfriend, Fern, and they were back together.

The twin he'd met just several months ago now felt like a trusted friend, someone Colt would turn to. For a lone wolf who could count on one hand those people, he now added two: Jake and Anna. He could likely add Sarah Mack Ford and her husband, Edmund, and he was sure he would as he got to know his birth mother better, too.

As he and Anna left, he knew he'd be back to visit soon and that Jake would come see him in Houston. They were forging their own relationship, and though they might not exactly think of themselves as brothers, they had a special connection that Colt felt deep inside.

As they headed back to town, Noah started fussing like crazy in his car seat. Colt pulled over to the side of the road and they both got out to investigate. With the twins rear-facing in their car seats, they couldn't see what was causing Noah the trouble.

The little guy was red-faced, yanking on his ear and crying. He looked absolutely miserable.

"Uh-oh. I wonder if he might have an ear infection," Anna said. "Why don't you take Nathaniel on a little adventure for the next hour while I bring Noah to the urgent-care clinic? I've passed it a bunch of times at the end of Blue Gulch Street. No appointment needed."

"Sure we shouldn't come with you?"

Anna shook her head. "We should probably keep Nathaniel away from anyone contagious at the clinic. I'll be fine on my own."

Colt nodded and they got back in and headed to town. He parked at the clinic, and Anna got out with Noah, taking the stroller so that she could easily wheel him back the half mile to the inn.

"Text me after you see the doc. If you want me to pick you up, just let me know."

Anna smiled. "I will."

She and Noah disappeared through the door, Colt immediately missing them. He was worried about Noah. But Anna said it was probably an ear infection, and he was pretty sure those were common in babies.

"We're on our own," he said to Nathaniel. "Know what I could go for? Lunch at Hurley's Homestyle Kitchen. Pulled-pork po'boy? Those spicy sweet potato fries? Sounds good, right?"

Nathaniel smiled.

"I thought you'd agree." This was good, actually. While Anna was away with Noah, he could read over the intel Harlan had texted this morning. Colt stopped by the inn to use the "business center" printer in the parlor. He'd buy the proprietor another pack of copier paper since the report was almost forty pages long.

Report in a manila envelope in one hand, Nathaniel in the other, Colt headed down to Hurley's. The restaurant was crowded, but there was a table for two that only one chair could fit, so Colt was able to bypass the other groups of two since a baby seat could still fit on one side of the table.

"Our lucky day, little guy," he said to Nathaniel, giving the baby a kiss on the cheek.

"Aww, so cute!" a smiling waitress said. He recognized her from his time in the kitchen; her name was Clementine. "Nice to see you again, Colt. And we know this cutie pie. Anna brought him and his twin when she volunteered a couple of days ago. His baby buddies miss him. Maybe I can sneak him into the kitchen to say hi after he eats."

Colt smiled. "Sure thing."

Another waitress took his order. The po'boy and fries for Colt and a jar of sweet potato baby food for Nathaniel. Colt put his report on the table beside his lunch, one eye on the devastating account of what had happened in the past week as Duvall and his thugs wreaked havoc all over Houston, and one eye on Nathaniel, who gobbled up every spoonful of his lunch.

Clementine returned to clear plates. "You're a great eater!" she said, kneeling down by Nathaniel. She waved a little stuffed monkey. "Remember how you loved playing with this last time you were here? Your buddy is in the kitchen. Want to come say hi?"

Nathaniel held his arms straight up, clearly wanting Clementine to pick him up.

Colt smiled. "Fine with me. I've got some heavy reading to do, so it's great timing."

"I'll bring him back in five minutes." She scooped up Nathaniel and took him into the kitchen.

Colt sipped his coffee and began reading carefully, highlighting and starring certain sections. Eliot Duvall was a monster and had to be stopped. Colt would go undercover as a high-end buyer of assault weapons and would meet with only Duvall to ostensibly ensure he wasn't walking into a trap, or no deal. He took notes on the weapons he needed to be an expert in, glancing at the photos Harlan had attached, including photos of Duvall and his top associates. It was as though he hadn't been away from the office, the field. Everything fell away but his work, the drive to learn everything about Duvall, to get him to the point where he could bust him. His mind reeling with all the information he'd taken in, his phone pinged with another text from Harlan. He was forwarding another report on the weapons Colt would "buy."

Colt got up and hurried back to the inn, wanting to print out the new report and study the photos and details. He sat in the parlor, reading through the material, his highlighter working furiously. He'd read through the first report again, all forty pages, then the second one again.

"Colt?"

He glanced up, and for a moment he didn't know where he was. Plush chocolate-brown sofa. Computer. Printer. Desks. He was in the parlor at the inn.

He shook his head to clear it.

"Anna! How's Noah?" He bolted up, rushing over to pick up his nephew. "So he has an ear infection?"

She stared at him, looking around the room. "Where's Nathaniel?"

Colt felt the blood drain from his face. "Oh, God. I—"

He'd left his baby nephew at Hurley's. He'd walked out without him.

He'd forgotten his seven-month-old nephew.

Colt rushed out the door, dimly aware that Anna was hurrying after him, Noah in her arms.

He raced up the porch steps to Hurley's and almost collided with people waiting for a table. He weaved between the crowd and into the kitchen.

"Oh, phew," Clementine said. "I brought Nathaniel back out to find you but didn't know where you were. I thought maybe you were in the restroom, but a half hour went by."

He closed his eyes in shame. "I'm so sorry. I—"

"No worries. You're here now." She held Nathaniel out to him, and for a moment he didn't feel like he deserved to take him.

He'd failed his nephew.

"Thanks for taking such good care of him. I got caught up in something and had to go back to the inn. I apologize."

"Really, no worries. All's well that ends well."

He stared at her. He'd said that exact thing to Anna when the guinea pig had been returned to him.

But this was very different. This was about a baby he'd forgotten. Because he'd been buried in his work, unable to think of anything or anyone else.

This was how it would be with Anna. He wouldn't hold back in the field because of her. He'd forget her entirely.

And she deserved better than that. Better than him.

He stalked out of the restaurant, Anna waiting for him with Noah.

"Colt? What happened?"

"Let's talk at the inn," he said, shifting Nathaniel in his arms.

They walked silently down the street to the inn. Once Nathaniel and Noah were in the playpen in Anna's room,

Noah looking much happier, Colt took Anna's hand and led her over to the far side of the room.

He explained what happened. "I was trying to figure out if I could do this, really do this, be the man you deserve. And I found out for sure just now that I'm not and that I can't be. I forgot my nephew, Anna. A baby. Yes, he was in good hands and safe. But what if I'd be somewhere else? What if I was in a restaurant where no one knew who I was? Anything could have happened."

"Colt, you're being too hard on yourself. Yes, you made a mistake. But I'm sure in the back of your mind you knew Nathaniel was with Clementine in the kitchen. You rushed out to print out the report and got lost in it. When I came back, you remembered Nathaniel and rushed to get him. He was just a few doors down in safe hands."

"I didn't remember. You asked where Nathaniel was. I didn't even realize he was gone until you asked."

The sympathy in her eyes bothered him. She should be angry and telling him off. "Oh, Colt."

"I found out who I really am today, Anna. I'm an FBI agent first. I don't want to be—I want to be with you. But my job will come first. That's who I am. When we get back to Houston, we'll be going our separate ways."

"Colt, I—"

"My mind is made up. In fact, I'd like to leave right now. Let's just get back. I don't want to be here anymore. You can stay in my guest room as the twins' nanny until tomorrow morning, when my sister and her husband will back."

She stared at him, a combination of hurt and anger flashing in her brown eyes. "I guess I'll start packing."

She glanced over at the playpen. Both babies had fallen asleep, Noah's little arm on his brother's tummy. "Let's at least wait until the twins wake up before we go."

"I need some air," Colt said and left, rushing out of the inn and down the street, no idea where he was headed.

He walked down the park at the end of the street and sat on a flat-topped rock, his head in his hands. How many times had his father forgotten to pick him up as he said he would, from sports practice or a game. *Sorry, champ, got caught up in work.* And instead of actually being sorry, his father was lost in thought of the job.

Colt would let down Anna time and again. And if he went with his heart and not his head and actually married her and had children? He'd disappoint them time and again.

Not going to happen. Because there could be no Colt and Anna in the first place.

Chapter Fourteen

The ride back to Houston was a silent, lonely three hours. At first, Anna had tried to talk to Colt. The circumstances had led to him forgetting about Nathaniel. The particular circumstances. Nathaniel had been in a safe place, which was why he hadn't been on Colt's mind.

He'd growled at her to stop making excuses for him. *There is no excuse for what I did*, he'd snapped, his hands gripping the steering wheel so tightly his knuckles were white.

"Okay, you forgot your nephew," she said. "Your mind was on your job, and you forgot your nephew. You made a mistake and I doubt it's one you'll make again."

"Damn straight," he said. "Because there won't be a next time. I won't babysit the twins on my own."

"Come on, Colt. You're never going to babysit your

nephews. You're never doing to do your sister the favor if she needs you?"

"No. And this conversation is over, Anna."

Brick wall. She wanted to scream in frustration. She'd been so close to reaching him. The lone wolf, who'd turned so tender last night and this morning, who'd changed her life forever. And now he was gone again.

When they arrived at Colt's condo, they each carried a baby from the garage, Colt taking Nathaniel.

"I'm so sorry I let you down," Colt whispered in the baby's ear. "You're precious and I was careless. I'm very sorry." He placed his nephew in the playpen and then went into his bedroom and closed the door, leaving his nanny to take care of the boys.

He'd never thought of her that way before. As his nanny. She'd been Anna, amazing Anna, full of surprises and bravery, a woman of many talents, including childcare. He was lucky to have known her. But it was time to say goodbye. In the morning, his sister and her husband would come pick up the twins, and then he'd offer to pay for a vacation rental for a week or two until Anna found her own place.

You don't have to go home, but you can't stay here— the words rang hollowly in his mind, his heart splitting in two.

He stewed for hours in his bedroom, not going over the reports on Duvall, not talking to Anna, not making these last hours with his nephews worthwhile. He laid on his bed, his hands behind his head, staring out at the night, the lights over Houston. He could just make out Anna singing a lullaby he recognized from his own childhood, one his mother had liked to sing.

There was a knock at his door. "It's open."

Anna came inside and sat down on the edge of the bed. "The boys are asleep. I just want to say one more thing. Will you listen?"

He nodded, keeping his gaze out the window.

"I love you, Colt. I don't judge you. I wish you didn't judge yourself so harshly. I'm standing here, offering you everything—the moon and the stars—and you're not taking it because you think you can't really have everything. But you can. Life is full of beautiful ups and horrible downs. You know this. You've lost your parents. I lost my parents. You've also found an amazing connection with your twin. And you escorted me into the world. Life is not going to be perfect. You're not going to be perfect. So please don't walk away from me, from us."

She was crying and he wanted to stand up and hold her, but he stayed where he was. He felt like lead, unable to move.

"I appreciate what you said, Anna. But I've made my decision. I'm leaving the day after Christmas on the case. And when I go, I'll be one-hundred-percent focused."

"You think I'm so forgettable?"

She had so much moxy that he found himself getting up and rushing over to her. He pulled her into his arms and held her tight. He held her and didn't want to let go, and she wrapped her arms around him.

"I'll never forget you. But I'm tucking you away. I'll think about you when I can, when I'm alone."

"Oh, Colt," she said, pulling away.

"My sister docks at the crack of dawn and will be here early, so we'd both better get some sleep." He needed her to leave or else he might break into a hundred pieces.

"So this is it?"

"It has to be, yes."

She wiped at her eyes and walked to the door. "Good night," she said.

"Goodbye."

Her face crumpled and she rushed out the door, closing it behind her. He heard her footsteps running to her bedroom, then the door close.

In all the worst moments of his life, none was worse than this.

"I've missed you little cherubs! Give Mama a big kiss!"

Colt's sister, Cathy, scooped up Noah and smothered him with kisses, getting giggles and Noah's chubby little arms around her neck. She handed him to her husband, who held him tight, and then Cathy picked up Nathaniel and kissed him at least twenty times all over his head and face.

"Cathy, Chris, this is Anna. She's been the twins' nanny since you left. I don't know what I would have done without her."

"So nice to meet you and thank you for taking such good care of our boys," Cathy said. "We desperately needed the vacation, but it was rough being away from the twins."

Chris nodded. "Every morning we'd wake up and think the twins were in the room next door, then we'd remember—we're on a cruise and we'd go take advantage of the all-you-can-eat buffet and we lay by the pools and we went to shows every night. It was great. But being home with these guys is better."

"They were angels," Anna said. "I'll miss them."

Cathy and Chris got the twins settled in their stroller, and Chris ran down to the garage with the car seats, then came back up and loaded his shoulders with the twins' bags.

"I owe you, my dear brother," Cathy said, flinging her arms around him. "Thank you for giving us this vacation."

"Honestly, my pleasure," Colt said. "But Anna gets the real credit. She did the heavy lifting."

Cathy squeezed Anna in a warm hug. "Thank you."

"Oh—Noah has a mild ear infection. Anna brought him to urgent care yesterday morning and he has antibiotics. The bottle is in the tote bag. He had his morning drops."

"Thanks again," Chris said, shaking Colt's hand. "You ever need a favor, you know who to call."

"And you'll come over tomorrow, right?" Cathy asked, heading to the door.

"I'll be over in the afternoon," Colt said. "I can't stay too long. I'm due in the field first thing the next morning."

"As long as you're with us for Christmas, even for an hour."

When the door closed behind them, Anna felt the absence of the twins so acutely.

"Feels so strange that Noah and Nathaniel aren't here," she said. "I feel like I should be checking on them or planning their dinner."

"It's a relief, though," Colt said, looking away.

She watched him for a moment, wondering if she should push it, if she should stay the night. But he was a closed door. Maybe he needed some time to let this blow over. Maybe he'd come for her in a few days or when his case was over.

Maybe this, maybe that. She couldn't live for maybes. If Colt was saying goodbye, she needed to let him go. She had her own life to live, dreams she intended to see come true. Not all of them would, as evidenced by the man standing in front of her. But some would. She'd work on those. *You can't control everything*, she wanted to yell at him. *Not yourself, even. And certainly not love.*

"Well, I guess the job has come to an end. If you'll give me a ride to my aunt and uncle's house in the Amish village, I'd appreciate it. I'll take a cab back to Houston after Christmas and start looking for an apartment then."

"Okay," he said. "Be right back." He disappeared into his bedroom and returned with what looked like a check. "For your hard work and a bonus."

"If I didn't need this to start my new life I wouldn't take it," she said. "Caring for those twins was a labor of love." She cleared her throat. "Last night I washed all the clothes I borrowed from your sister and put them back where I found them. I packed this morning, so I'm ready to go."

He stared at her, hard, but only nodded.

They were silent on the twenty-minute drive to the Amish village. Finally, he pulled up alongside her aunt and uncle's house, and the familiarity was comforting, but she felt so removed from this place, this village and the lifestyle, that it no longer felt like home.

She turned to face him. "Colt, thank you for everything. *Everything.* And like I assured you, I'm still very glad you were my first. With the man I love and will always treasure."

He glanced at her and squeezed her hand and released it, and she knew it was time to go.

Getting out of his car and walking away was the hardest thing she'd ever done.

Chapter Fifteen

Colt watched Anna walk toward the front door, his heart splitting again. The door opened and her aunt and cousin rushed out to greet her and wrap her in hugs. Colt put his sunglasses back on and quickly backed out of the drive and went up the long dirt road that led out of the community.

Sharp pokes in the region of his heart had him pulling over to the side of the road to take a breath and collect himself.

He loved her and he was leaving her. That made no damn sense. And yet it did. It took everything in him to start the car and keep driving away, farther and farther from his Anna. From his heart.

He wasn't in any shape to drive into Houston traffic, so he parked in Grass Creek and got out of the car, needing a strong cup of coffee. There were Amish people here and there, heading toward the market. He could believe that the woman he just spent a week with in Blue Gulch had been one of them not very long ago.

He continued walking, stopping in the coffee shop for a cappuccino, then passed the pet shop where Harlan had bought the guinea pig that had started everything. He backed up.

Wait a minute.

Another black-and-white guinea pig was in the window with two friends, a cinnamon-and-white long-haired guinea pig and another that was mostly white. His heart squeezed at the sight of the black-and-white critter. *Because of your kind, I fell in love and now I'm a mess*, he said silently, pointing a finger at the guinea pig in the window.

And before he could stop himself, he went in and bought it. And a cage. And wood shavings. And food. And a hidey tunnel. And a how-to-take-care-of-your-new-guinea-pig book. Not for himself. As a Christmas gift for Anna's little cousin, Sadie.

He drove back to the Amish village and parked by Anna's aunt and uncle's house. Before he could even open the door, they all came out, Sadie's red pigtails flying behind her as she rushed out the door, the group of them staring at the Englisher in the FBI-agent shades. He took them off and put them in his pocket.

Anna's expression was so full of pain and longing that he almost rushed to her to hold her, to assure her that he felt as horribly as she did, but what could they do? This was how it had to be.

He cleared his throat. "I have a Christmas present for Sadie, if it's all right with you, Kate and Eli."

Sadie's eyes widened. "A gift for me?" She looked at her parents, waiting for their approval. Or lack of it.

"Well, go see what it is," Eli said.

Sadie ran over to the car and looked in the passenger seat. She covered her mouth with her hands and tears began pouring down her cheeks. She stood there and sobbed.

"Good Lord, what is it?" Kate said, rushing over with her husband.

Anna trailed behind them. She peered in the car and Colt could see the tears misting in her beautiful driftwood-colored eyes.

"Can I keep him, *Mamm* and *Daed*?" Sadie asked, the pleading in her voice almost unbearable. Tears still streamed down her cheeks.

"If you want the critter, why are you sobbing?" her father asked.

"Because I want him so bad." She dropped down on her knees, burying her face in her hands.

"Oh, for heaven's sake, *kinder*," Eli said, pulling her up. "Go get your guinea pig. He's probably hungry."

Sadie stared at her father, her face brightening. She wrapped her arms around him, then her mother, then Anna, then Colt, catching him by surprise.

"If it's okay with you, Mr. Colt, I'm going to name him Agent Sparkles."

"Agent Sparkles?" Kate said. "Is that an English name?"

Colt glanced at Anna. She smiled, then laughed. He smiled back, wanting to take her in his arms and hold her so badly it hurt, but he stayed where he was.

"Agent Sparkles is a good English name," Anna said. "If that's all right with you, *Onkel* and *Aenti*."

Eli raised an eyebrow. "Well, it's Sadie's present so she can name the cute guinea pig whatever she wants."

"There's a big bag of wood shavings for his cage. And in the other bag is everything you need, plus a book on how to take care of a guinea pig."

"Thank you, Agent Colt," Sadie said. "Thank you so much. You can come visit him whenever you want. I can't wait to read the book."

Colt kneeled down in front of Sadie. "You're very welcome. And Merry Christmas."

"Merry Christmas," Sadie said. "Will you help me carry him into my room?" she asked her parents.

Eli took the cage while Kate took the big sack of shavings and Sadie carried the bag with the food, the tunnel and the book.

"That was very thoughtful of you, Colt," Anna said when her family had gone inside the house. "But that's the Colt Asher I know. Not the one who's afraid of what might happen. Or afraid to accept that he's human."

"I love you too much to let you down," he said.

"You're letting me down anyway," she said, rushing over to him. She slipped both hands to his face, holding his gaze. "Do you understand that? You're letting me down by walking away. I'm telling you I'm in this. I know who you are. I know what you do. Based on everything you know about me, are you telling me I can't handle it?"

"*I* can't handle it," he said.

"So we're in love but you're walking away. Oh, that makes sense."

"Goodbye, Anna," he said, then got in his car and drove away, tears stinging his eyes.

* * *

Colt spent the rest of the day Christmas shopping for his sister, Chris and the twins, constantly seeing gifts he knew Anna would love. He had to stop thinking about her. He had to put his mind on hyperfocus. Christmas. His family. Making calls to Blue Gulch to say "Merry Christmas" and "Happy New Year." Then it was the Duvall crime organization for the foreseeable future.

He tossed and turned all night, unable to stop thinking about her, wondering what she was doing, what her Christmas Eve meal had been, what she'd gotten Sadie as a gift.

In the morning, he got up early and worked out in the condo's gym, then took a long hot shower and carted all the presents to his car for the short drive over to his sister's.

He'd bought the twins way too much. Something called Jumperoos that hung from a doorway and let them bounce-jump to their hearts' content. Two exersaucers. Two baby-sized leather bomber jackets that he couldn't resist. He'd gotten Cathy tickets to a concert he knew she'd want, and Chris tickets to the hockey championships. They'd gotten him flying lessons, something he'd always wanted to do. Noah and Nathaniel had gotten him a joint gift, a T-shirt that said Texas's Best Uncle.

He froze, the navy T-shirt limp in his hand in his sister's family room.

Cathy frowned. "Colt? You hate it? It's adorable."

Colt stood up and walked over to the sliding glass door to the backyard, where Chris was playing peekaboo with the twins in their baby swings as he pushed one at a time. "It's very cute. But it's not true. I'm the *worst* uncle, Cathy."

"What are you talking about? How happy do those twins look to you?"

He turned back to Cathy and launched into the whole story. Starting with Harlan and Sparkles. Explaining the whole mess with leaving Nathaniel in the restaurant. And ending with breaking up with Anna, who he loved like crazy.

"Oh, Colt. You think I never left one of the twins somewhere by accident? I once left Noah in a shopping cart in the supermarket while I loaded my car with bags of groceries, then drove halfway home before I realized he was still in the cart in the store vestibule. It had been raining that day so I figured I'd leave him for a minute while I ran to the car, parked right where I could see the cart. I completely forgot to go back."

He stared at her. "What? Really? That's terrible."

She lightly punched him in the arm. "I know. But it happens. Only that once. But it happens. Chris admitted he'd once left Noah at his best friend's house, thinking both boys were in their car seats. He'd gotten all the way home and didn't realize it until he saw the empty car seat."

Huh. He hadn't expected to hear any of that. "I felt like hell about it. To me it means I can't make everything in my life fit. If I want to be a good agent, I need to be hyperfocused on being an agent. I can't be in love. I can't be thinking of my girlfriend finding out I'm injured or dead. I need to be one-hundred-percent on the job."

"Being one-hundred-percent focused on something will just burn you out. And one night, you'll come home from a case that's done a number on you and you'll have nothing and no one. You'll be alone in the truest sense of the world, Colt. Self-imposed loneliness."

He shrugged. "It's worked so far."

"Oh, really? What about Anna? The woman you fell madly in love with?"

"I don't know how to have everything, Cath. I don't want her to get hurt."

"Or maybe *you* don't," Cathy said pointedly. "Dad was always disappointing us, making promises and not keeping them. I think we both learned not to expect, not to hope, not to dream. And how we lost them… I was afraid to love anyone after that. Even you, Colt. And we're all we had."

They'd both been distant with each other after they lost their parents. Defense mechanisms. But the birth of the twins had brought them closer. Thank God.

"I tried not to fall for Chris when we met," Cathy continued. "But he kept at me until he broke down my defenses. Like Anna did for you."

"And so what is it like?" Colt asked. "How do you give everything your all?"

"It took me a while to figure out how to make all the important pieces of my life fit. How to have time for Chris, how to give the babies the time each need individually and together, how to have time for myself. How to have time for my brother. I take yoga every day, Colt. Every day without fail. And while I'm there, I'm focused on twisting my body into uncomfortable positions. I don't think of the boys. I don't think of Chris. I just breathe."

Colt nodded, a tiny crack breaking open inside him.

His sister's words were getting through—or maybe they were just making sense to him in terms of her life.

"Colt, do you know why I left the boys with you?"

"Because you had no choice."

"Are you kidding? Chris's parents are a half hour away and they're a little spacey, but they could have taken the twins for the week—and would have. But I wanted you to take Noah and Nathaniel. I wanted you to know them in a way you only can if you spend twenty-four/seven with them. I want you to be close to them, Colt, and I saw the opportunity and took it. You mad?"

"Are you kidding? My life changed because of it. I fell in love with my Amish nanny—who is now formerly Amish."

"Go get her, Colt. Put both of you out of your misery on Christmas day for God's sake."

Colt smiled. "Why is my younger sister so much wiser than I am?"

"It's the woman thing," she said. "We're just smarter in all ways."

"Don't I know it." He hugged her tight, kissed his nephews and ran out the door.

Anna was up early on Christmas day, working in the barn on painting some wooden dolls that Kate wanted to give her neighbors, who had a houseful of little girls. She left their faces unpainted, as was the Amish style. The girls would see who they wanted, who they envisioned in the dolls.

She'd spent Christmas Eve with her family, trying to forget her broken heart, trying not to think of the man she loved and missed so much she couldn't breathe.

Being home was a comfort, but at the same time, this village wasn't home anymore. She belonged in the English world and tomorrow, she'd be moving to Houston, staying in a hotel until she found an apartment of her own. She planned to get a job as a nurse's aide at the hospital where she'd said goodbye to both her parents, and hopefully, she would be accepted into Houston College and the department of nursing. It helped to think of her plan, her goals. But then her pain would sneak up on her and knock her to her knees.

She missed him so much and she'd just seen him yesterday. Sadie hadn't stopped talking about Agent Sparkles or how kind Colt was and how she'd never forget what he did for her.

Anna wouldn't, either.

Kate had asked if there was something between her and the FBI agent, and Anna had told her aunt the truth: yes, but it was over now. Her *aenti* had hugged her tight and said she was sorry and that maybe it would all work out.

Anna wasn't one to give up on hope, but Colt wouldn't even be around starting tomorrow—and he'd vowed not to think of Anna when he was at work and out in the field. It would be out of sight, out of mind, and by the time the case was over, she'd be a distant memory. *Remember that time you fell for the Amish woman on her* rumspringa? *Crazy, huh?*

Tears poked at her eyes and she forced herself to focus on finishing the last doll. She'd just set her to dry when she heard the sound of a car on gravel outside the barn.

A car. On Christmas day.

Colt?

She bolted up and looked out the barn window. It was Colt!

Please be here to say you've come to your senses. Please don't be here to say a final goodbye. I can't take it.

She walked outside, realizing he stood in the same spot he did when she'd first laid eyes on him a week ago.

"Merry Christmas," he said.

Dear God, was that why he was here? To wish her a happy holiday. She didn't think she could bear this another moment. "Merry Christmas," she said after a long pause.

He dropped down on one knee, holding a little black box in his hand. A ring box.

She gasped, her hand flying to her mouth.

He opened the box. A beautiful diamond ring glittered in the morning sun. "I bought this ring in the jewelry shop in Blue Gulch the day I played basketball with Devin and helped him realize a few truths. I realized a few truths that day, too. The biggest one being that I loved you, Anna. I knew I wanted you in my life forever. So I marched into the jewelry shop and bought the one ring that I thought you'd love more than any other. And then I forgot my nephew in the restaurant, and I buried the ring in my luggage."

She was trying very hard not to burst into tears. She really didn't want to distract him from continuing.

"All I need to know is that I love you more than anything, Anna. Anything. Will you marry me?"

She flung herself at him, knocking him over onto the grass. "Yes. Yes. Yes!"

They sat up and he faced her, sliding the ring on her

finger. "I'm sorry I had a crisis of…I don't know— faith in myself, you, humanity. Everything. I love you, Anna. I can't live without you. That's what I know."

For a moment she was speechless and could barely find her breath. Her wish had come true. Her Christmas wish. Her lifetime wish. "I feel the same way."

He held her tight. "I also need you to know that I *am* going undercover tomorrow. I don't know how long I'll be gone. But I need to get Duvall off the street. I need to be an agent. It's who I am."

"I know. Just like I need to become a trauma nurse. I've got my own life, Colt. And while you're doing your thing, I'll be doing mine."

He pulled her up, wrapping her in his arms. "We're in this together, Anna. I don't have to be a lone wolf. I finally understand that. We're a *we*."

She was so happy she could barely find her breath. "I love you, Colt Asher."

"I love you," he said, kissing her full on the lips. "Merry Christmas, Anna."

"The merriest," she said.

Epilogue

It was a beautiful day for a wedding. The first day of spring was bright and sunny, and the forecast was for a warm seventy-two degrees. The sky was blue without a hint of clouds, and there wasn't a drop of humidity in the air. "A good hair day," as Anna's new English friends would say.

The entire village had been invited to Anna and Colt's wedding, taking place in the field adjacent to her house. Everyone had gathered, including her former best friend, Caleb, who was now married himself to a lovely Amish woman, and Jordan Lapp and his fiancée, Abigail, to erect the tent and set up the tables. The Amish had cooked all the food and the best of the singers among them would provide song, if not music.

Anna had surprised herself by wanting to be married in her village. She felt it was honoring her heritage, who she'd been, as she set out on this new journey of who she was. There were a few conditions on both sides—the bishop had drawn the line at music, but singing was fine, of course. Anna had insisted photographs be allowed and a videographer, too.

Anna had informed Eli and Kate that she'd invited her cousin Mara and her boyfriend and that the two of them were to sit among the family, be welcomed back for the day, and treated with love and respect. Tears had come to Eli's eyes; Mara was his niece, who he'd continued to pray for, and the bishop had agreed since he'd never known Mara anyway and hardly anyone remembered her except her own family, and Anna, Eli, Kate and Sadie were it. Over the past few months, Anna had spent more time with Mara and she was thrilled her cousin would be part of her wedding day.

Now, Anna was putting on the final touches in her bedroom in her house, which she'd donated to the village for use as a temporary housing for anyone who might need it, including those unsure of where their hearts lay, with the Amish or the English. She glanced at herself in the standing full-length mirror that she'd brought over and smuggled inside for the occasion.

She'd driven back to Blue Gulch to buy her wedding dress, which she'd seen hanging in the bridal salon window during the week she'd spent there with Colt. It was a combination of her old and new life. There was something Victorian about the gown, yet princess-like at the same time. It was high-necked with slightly puffed long sleeves, yet lacy and delicate. She felt like a forties movie star in it. Her hair was pulled back, and she wore light makeup and beautiful *peau-de-soie* pumps. Her aunt Kate and her sister-in-law-to-be, Cathy, had helped her get ready. She and Cathy had gotten close since Christmas, shopping, going to movies, and gossiping—gently—about Colt, whom they both loved dearly. Anna loved getting to spend so much time with Noah and Nathaniel, who would be ring bearers at the wedding. The thought of them in their little tuxedos made her burst into a smile.

She glanced out the window to see Colt deep in conversation with her uncle. Her groom wore a very sharp tuxedo and looked so handsome her knees wobbled. She smiled as she saw Jake and Emma Morrow arrive with baby Violet and the Fords, Sarah and Edmund. Cathy walked up to Jake and Sarah and hugged them both. Colt had invited the Morrows and Fords to their condo a few months ago for dinner and a show, putting them up in a swanky hotel. The six of them had had a great time, and Anna could see how moved Colt was at having his sister and his twin and birth mother all together.

Separately, she and Colt had found their families growing, and now their families would be uniting, growing even bigger.

"Ready?" her *aenti* asked, poking her head in the room, a beaming Sadie, her flower girl, at her side. Sadie had asked if Agent Sparkles could come to the wedding, his cage under her chair, and Anna said she couldn't imagine the dear guinea pig not being a guest at her wedding.

Oh, yes. "Ready."

Outside, Anna looked at the rows of chairs, at these people she loved and people she would come to know. There was Colt's boss, Harlan Holtzman, and his wife, and a few of his fellow FBI agents. Colt had indeed gotten Eliot Duvall off the street and behind bars, and it had taken him less than a week. For two days after, Colt and Anna hadn't left his condo, snuggling in bed, having Thai takeout, making love, watching movies. She was so happy it seemed like a dream.

And now she was about to marry the man she loved. Tomorrow morning, she would wake up married to Colt, a wedding band on her finger, and they'd fly off to Rome, Italy, for their honeymoon. All the pasta she wanted for two weeks. She couldn't imagine having any more wishes to make at the Trevi Fountain; all her wishes had come true. Though maybe she'd make a wish for a little Colt or a little Anna to come into their lives when they were ready—twins, she thought with a grin. In September, she would start classes at Houston College, majoring in nursing, so they'd put off starting a family for a few years.

But the best part of it all: she and Colt *were* in this together. Every step of the way.

Her uncle walked her down the aisle, English-style, to her handsome groom, her past and present meeting for the future of her dreams.

* * * * *

Meg Maxwell will return to
Mills & Boon Cherish in April 2018 writing
under her real name, Melissa Senate!

In the meantime, be sure to catch other books in the
HURLEY'S HOMESTYLE KITCHEN *series:*

CHARM SCHOOL FOR COWBOYS
THE COOK'S SECRET INGREDIENT
THE COWBOY'S BIG FAMILY TREE
THE DETECTIVE'S 8LB, 10 OZ SURPRISE
A COWBOY IN THE KITCHEN

Available now from Mills & Boon Cherish!

MILLS & BOON®

Cherish™

EXPERIENCE THE ULTIMATE RUSH OF FALLING IN LOVE

A sneak peek at next month's titles...

In stores from 16th November 2017:

- **Married Till Christmas** – Christine Rimmer *and*
  Christmas Bride for the Boss – Kate Hardy
- **The Maverick's Midnight Proposal** – Brenda Harlen
  and **The Magnate's Holiday Proposal** –
  Rebecca Winters

In stores from 30th November 2017:

- **Yuletide Baby Bargain** – Allison Leigh *and*
  The Billionaire's Christmas Baby – Marion Lennox
- **Christmastime Courtship** – Marie Ferrarella *and*
  Snowed in with the Reluctant Tycoon – Nina Singh

Just can't wait?
Buy our books online before they hit the shops!
www.millsandboon.co.uk

Also available as eBooks.

MILLS & BOON®

EXCLUSIVE EXTRACT

With just days until Christmas, gorgeous but bewildered billionaire Max Grayland needs hotel maid Sunny Raye's help caring for his baby sister Phoebe. She agrees – only if they spend Christmas with her family!

Read on for a sneak preview of
THE BILLIONAIRE'S CHRISTMAS BABY

'Miss Raye, would you be prepared to stay on over Christmas?'

Oh, for heaven's sake…

To miss Christmas… Who were they kidding?

'No,' she said blankly. 'My family's waiting.'

'But Mr Grayland's stranded in an unknown country, staying in a hotel for Christmas with a baby he didn't know existed until yesterday.' The manager's voice was urbane, persuasive, doing what he did best. 'You must see how hard that will be for him.'

'I imagine it will be,' she muttered and clung to her chocolates. And to her Christmas. 'But it's…'

Max broke in. 'But if there's anything that could persuade you… I'll double what the hotel will pay you. Multiply it by ten if you like.'

Multiply by ten… If it wasn't Christmas…

But it was Christmas. Gran and Pa were waiting. She had no choice.

But other factors were starting to niggle now. Behind Max, she could see tiny Phoebe lying in her too-big cot. She'd pushed herself out of her swaddle and was waving her tiny hands in desperation. Her face was red with screaming.

She was so tiny. She needed to be hugged, cradled, told all was right with her world. Despite herself, Sunny's heart twisted.

But to forgo Christmas? *No way.*

'I can't,' she told him, still hugging her chocolates. But then she met Max's gaze. This man was in charge of his world but he looked...desperate. The pressure in her head was suddenly overwhelming.

And she made a decision. What she was about to say was ridiculous, crazy, but the sight of those tiny waving arms, that red, desperate face was doing something to her she didn't understand and the words were out practically before she knew she'd utter them.

'Here's my only suggestion,' she told them. 'If you really do want my help... My Gran and Pa live in a big old house in the outer suburbs. It's nothing fancy; in fact it's pretty much falling down. It might be dilapidated but it's huge. So no, Mr Grayland, I won't spend Christmas here with you, but if you're desperate, if you truly think you can't manage Phoebe alone, then you're welcome to join us until you can make other arrangements. You can stay here and take care of Phoebe yourself, you can make other arrangements or you can come home with me. Take it or leave it.'